Our Plan To Save the World

and other stories of false starts, dead ends, detours, and determined people looking for their happy ending.

by Nancy Kay Clark, Phyllis Humby,
Michael Joll, Steve Nelson, and Frank T. Sikora

Published by Lulu.com, U.S.A.

Editing: Nancy Kay Clark & Steve Nelson
Art direction: Frank T. Sikora
Layout: Nancy Kay Clark & Doug Bennet
Cover illustration: Susan Tolonen

ISBN 978-1-387-52018-3

The Almost True History of Our Anthology
Frank T. Sikora

Our Plan to Save The World is not the anthology I intended to produce. Yes, it contains a wonderfully diverse selection of stories, with each writer bringing a unique, authentic, and honest voice to his or her work. Even after numerous readings, these stories continue to affect me. I could just say I'm proud of the collection, but honestly, and thankfully, I can say it has exceeded my original vision.

My original goals were modest. First and foremost, I wanted a legacy collection: stories that represented the best work of writers I enjoyed, that deserved to be preserved, and not just on some obscure server, but in an old-school, print, sit on the bookshelf collection (but yes, an e-book version will also be available!). I hoped that the anthology would give these writers a much-deserved, larger audience.

This legacy collection idea had been roaming around my grey matter for a few years, but it kicked into drive shortly after my father died in July of 2016, leaving me the only surviving member of my immediate family. One of my proudest memories was handing my father an anthology collection that contained two of the first stories I had published. The first thing my father, a World War II veteran and child of the Great Depression, asked was how much I got paid. When I told him it was a whopping seventy-five dollars, he smiled and said, "That's barely a week's worth of groceries." Then he quickly added, "Are the stories any good?"

I didn't answer, nor did I inquire whether he liked them. I didn't want to know. All writers, well 99.9 percent of them, have learned to live with rejection. Still, each time a story of mine was published in print, I sent him a copy. He didn't have access to the stories published online, and the validity of works published this way was lost on him. Living as if it were 1965, he didn't have a computer, balanced his checkbook manually, paid with cash, kept an emergency $1000 in a metal box in the closet, and read the daily paper each morning.

Cleaning out his possessions after he died, during that same awful July, I found that collection with my first two stories, plus all the others, in a drawer that also contained his U.S. Army discharge papers, family birth certificates, and photos of my mother and brother. I wished he'd had access to all my stories. That's when my plan to leave a printed legacy in the form of this anthology crystalized.

*

Two things happened during the anthology's development—one good and one worrisome. First, the worrisome: As soon as we started the story selection process, I began to have my doubts. It wasn't the quality of the stories. They were all good and covered a wide range of styles and genres (literary, historical, psychological suspense, and speculative). Many had won awards. But I began to wonder: why, amid the multitudes of publications released every year, would anyone care about this collection?

The good news, that eased my fears, came as we were completing the story selection process and Nancy Kay Clark, a wonderful editor, writer, and all-around story goddess, recognized that, besides the fact that a majority of the protagonists are women, there was a connective thread binding our stories into a cohesive whole. The characters in this anthology share a sense of displacement, uncertain of their roles in society. Young or old, they desire connection. They demand lives with purpose. Meaning. Perhaps even a happy ending. They all want a home in this wonderfully wide and terrifying world.

*

A few words about the stories:

While I love all the works, and am proud to have mine in print alongside them, a number of stories inspired this collection.

First, the twist at the end of Steve Nelson's story bearing the anthology's title changed my stubborn belief that such endings are inherently false and cheap. Instead, this ending is artistically and emotionally satisfying. Furthermore, this story not only opens this collection, it sends the anthology's characters on their individual journeys, and while not all the journeys are successful, or morally righteous, or likeable, all are worth reading about.

Nancy's "The Naming of Things" is one of the finest fantasy shorts I have read, and any story that contains the fabulous line, "I was sitting on the roof pondering motion and gravity," deserves to be read by as many folks as possible.

One of the original criteria for the anthology was that all stories had to be previously published. But when Phyllis Humby submitted "The Final Curtain," the committee voted on including it over her previously published, award-winning selections. Those other works were wonderful, but this story lingers, seeping deep into one's emotional consciousness, and isn't that what matters? I was deeply affected by and still think about the frightful yet emotionally satisfying decision the group of women in this story make.

In another one of my favorites, "The Song of Solomon" by Michael Joll, two sisters struggle with a family legacy all the more horrific because of the silence the family legacy demands. This story touched a deep emotional nerve for me, but I believe its appeal is universal.

So, no, *Our Plan to Save The World* is not the anthology I envisioned. It is more—more diverse in character, genre, and style, yet still thematically cohesive. This happy surprise wouldn't have come to pass without all of the contributors' help and expertise: Nancy's editorial guidance, Steve's editing and proofreading, Michael's research, and Phyllis's marketing efforts.

I also want to thank Nancy and her husband Doug Bennet for producing the book, Susan Tolonen for illustrating the (awesome) cover, and the team of outside proofreaders for ensuring a consistent and professional production.

I believe we have produced an anthology of stories worth reading and preserving. As writers and readers, we know there is only one tried and true way to save the world—one story, one person at a time.

*

A word about spelling: Since we are a cross-border anthology, we decided not to be rigid when it came to spelling and style. Believing that language and even spelling reflect place and time, we allowed setting to dictate whether American or Canadian spelling should be used.

Nancy Kay Clark

After many years as a magazine writer and editor, Toronto-based Nancy Kay Clark began to write fiction, but couldn't settle on what kind—literary, children's, sci-fi or speculative (so she writes all four). Her short fiction has been featured in *Neo Opsis* magazine. She launched her own online literary magazine, CommuterLit.com, in 2010 (it's still going strong); and in 2018 will publish a middle-grade novel, *The Prince of Sudland*. You can find her stories on CommuterLit, and on Wattpad.

Phyllis Humby

Phyllis Humby's award-winning short stories have been described as scheming, twisted, and spooky. That's just the way she likes it. In addition to her passion for writing suspense thrillers from her rural Ontario home, she pens a monthly column, *Up Close and Personal*, for *First Monday* magazine. Columns and more at phyllishumby.blogspot.com

Michael Joll

Michael Joll has called Brampton, Ontario (just north of Toronto), home for more than forty years. The city's inhabitants, mainly immigrants and their children, provide fertile ground from which to build the characters in his stories. A retired police officer, his fingerprints and mug shot are still on file with the RCMP (Royal Canadian Mounted Police). His first collection of short stories, *Perfect Execution*, was published in 2017. He currently serves as the president of the Brampton Writers' Guild.

Steve Nelson

Steve Nelson lives in Chicago. He earned his PhD in Creative Writing from the University of Wisconsin-Milwaukee and has been published in *The Rambler*, *Storyglossia*, *eye-rhyme*, *The Absinthe Literary Review*, and elsewhere. His essay "Mind Wide Open" is included in the anthology, *The Runner's High: Illumination and Ecstasy in Motion*. "Night at the Store" was published in *Phantasmagoria* and nominated for a Pushcart Prize.

Frank T. Sikora

Frank T. Sikora is a graphic artist, writer, substitute teacher, and track coach. He lives in Waterford, Wisconsin with his wife, Holly, an English teacher. His work has been published online and in print in Canada and the U.S. Every once in a while one of his flash fiction pieces will win an award, which his wife will acknowledge with a smile and a comment, such as, "It still needs a middle, sweetheart."

Set off on the search...

"the chill of autumn coming"

Maranda on Fire

Our Plan to Save the World
Steve Nelson

We waited until everyone was asleep; then we drove all night to Chicago. My mom wouldn't know her van had disappeared until she woke at seven to get my sis ready for summer school. That first day, I worried about Sis making it to class on time, but Jenny said, "The world will go on without us." I figured she was right. I would've liked to have kept going. Arizona, I guess. Maybe California. But we didn't have the money for gas, and I figured it was best to let Jenny do the planning. She was the reason we went. I thought making the decisions might brighten her up. I never would have thought to go without her, but it's true I didn't like it when my mom said, "You're spending too much time with Jenny," or "I don't like the way you look at her." Sometimes my mom said nothing. When she looked at me, I got the feeling that, at fifteen, I was getting a little too big for her house.

The first few days, Jenny and I stayed close to the van. Moved it from spot to spot. When we were out, we kept walking, trying to blend in. When we saw nobody paid attention to us, or anyone else, we relaxed. We explored the lake and sat on the beach, hiked through the bird sanctuary, looked over the boats in the marina, watched the skateboarders do their tricks. We spent our money on bananas and bread and peanut butter from Aldi, and we pulled the wrapped food out of the dumpsters at the McDonalds or Sonic. Some nights we volunteered at the church on the corner to pass out food. That way, we got to eat too. The first time I said we should just go eat, but Jenny said we'd be less suspicious this way. She was right.

Jenny was hotter than blazes for a while. Boy, we steamed up that van, though we never got to where I thought we might. Before we left, we had joked and teased one another that if we ever had some real privacy, we could...

When we had the chance, it just didn't feel right. Before long, she ran out of her perfume, and we couldn't shower. She started to smell like underarms and French fries, which didn't exactly put me in the mood. So it was no great sacrifice. I knew I was ahead of the game. She took long walks along the lakefront all the way up to where the big apartments came to the water. She said she wanted to be alone, but I followed behind. At times, I wondered what she was thinking, but mostly I walked and kept her in view.

Some mornings while Jenny slept, I went to the soccer fields to sprint back and forth until I felt like I might pass out. Then I slowly weaved like I was dribbling the ball down field. I hardly ever imagined shooting for goals, because making good passes was more satisfying for me. I knew soccer season would start soon, and I wouldn't be there. I didn't love it that much, but when I played I forgot about everything else. I'd miss that. Even though I was tired, living like we were, I never got that nice spent feeling that only came after a long practice or a game—when I felt beat but refreshed. I tried on those mornings, but I never got there.

One day, Jenny said she wanted to go to church. Not to eat, but to go inside and pray. We'd never done this before, and I said I wasn't expecting much, but okay. As we walked over, Jenny wouldn't look at me, and she mumbled to herself. I thought she was warming up for how to pray and what to ask for. It didn't matter though because we heard gunshots coming from the church when we were a block away, then saw a car come speeding past us. Figuring it was the shooters, I ducked to hide, but Jenny kept walking. When I caught up to her at the corner, we stood and saw four bodies bleeding and groaning on the church steps. We smelled the powder from the guns. It took a couple minutes for the sirens to follow. We'd seen guys around the neighborhood before who looked like they might be in gangs, but we had never seen any guns or shootings. We turned around and walked back to the van. We tried talking about it a few times, but never got anywhere.

On the weekends, big Mexican families grilled in the park and played terrible volleyball games on saggy nets in the dirt. They didn't care they were bad, and they were happy to just be out there. We went through and took in all the smells from the barbecues, saw the meats smoking on the grills, and heard the sounds of the pop cans opening. It was kind of a mix between torture and satisfaction. Torture when we walked through, but afterwards, it was almost like, "Hey, that was pretty good."

Jenny spent some afternoons sitting under trees while she scribbled down poems that she wouldn't let me read. Then we went to the marina, and she threw them in the water. She smiled, so I didn't care. A few nights, it got so hot we took a blanket and slept out in the hollows of the golf course. It was nice to wake up with the cool dewy grass, to see the sun coming up, and to hear the birds.

They found us after about a month. A guy walked past our van. He headed towards Starbucks and recognized us from the news. I read in the paper afterwards that he had seen the Michigan plates, and that Jenny's parents and my mom had been on the news asking about us. I hadn't figured they would go on television, because they wouldn't have known where we were. We could've been in Canada, Cleveland, or anywhere a tank of gas and a couple hundred bucks could get us. But I didn't mind. The police in Chicago were nice enough, and they gave us pizza and Cokes. I knew we couldn't be in too much trouble, because we were both under sixteen and hadn't hurt anybody. I asked them about the shooting at the church, but they wouldn't tell me much except to say no one had died.

The police from Michigan picked us up, and Jenny and I got to sit together in the back seat all the way home. My mom hugged me, and I told her I was sorry if she was scared. She said she was, but knew I'd be okay. Jenny's parents were crying when we got there. They seemed like tears of joy. Her dad came over to me, and he looked like he was going to give me a friendly handshake. He squeezed it with all his might and whispered, "You're going to pay for this." And then he backed off and smiled at me again when everyone could see. I didn't care. Like I said, it was all Jenny's idea in the first place. Actually, it was her second idea. The first one was to kill herself, and when I told her it was no good, she said, "Well maybe we could just run away." And so that's what we did.

Hey Miles, What's the Plan?

Frank T. Sikora

Miles Edwards, 67, former outdoor life editor of the *Bismarck Tribune* and part-time substitute schoolteacher, entered room 134 of Bismarck High. Murmurs of recognition greeted him, punctuated by Stephanie Riley's squeal and then shout of "Miles! Yes!" While the students laughed, Stephanie poked her friend, Anna, and said, "See, I told you it would be him."

Miles waved and closed the door, temporarily sealing out the chaos behind him. As he walked to the podium, he thought, I should just go home. I should go home before the next onslaught of probability waves. I should go home before I break down in front of the kids.

When Miles entered the school that morning, his gift—the ability to see the multitude of reality states and probable futures of an individual—had again turned dark and pessimistic. As he studied the kids' faces, he saw only lives of despair, futures filled with tragedy. Lord, he wondered, what happened to the days when I not only saw the darkness in their lives but also the light?

He couldn't leave, though. He and his wife needed the money. At 67, his job prospects had been reduced to substitute teaching or delivering newspapers. His 401(k) decimated, he and his wife needed the $80 per day to supplement their Social Security. Miles took little comfort knowing that in all his realities, the results were similar. The worldwide economic downturn raged across all his existences.

"Good morning, ladies and gentlemen," Miles said. The students playfully snickered when he wrote his name on the whiteboard with the honorific, "Mr." To the kids, he was Miles, and had been since the first time he subbed for Ms. Klusmeyer's freshman English class. Stephanie had asked if she could call him "Miles," and looking out at the plump and sweet Ms. Riley, he had said, "Sure." Now he was known as Miles, nothing more.

Miles gazed at the students, starting on his left. It was a relief to see Janet Hastings looking well. He recalled seeing nothing but doomed futures for her the last time he'd taught: childhood leukemia, traffic accidents, drugs, and poverty. It was as if the universes had a malicious vendetta against the poor girl. He quickly turned away, afraid to look closer. For now, he could convince himself she would be safe.

Stephanie raised her hand. "Hey Miles, what's the plan?"

When Miles turned toward the student, one of his favorites, a sickness slithered in his gut. He hadn't noticed before, but the young redhead wore a Goth-inspired ensemble: black scarf, black T-shirt, black socks, shoes, and pants—an unusual colour palette for the girl whose current reality states rarely involved anything more serious than classroom anxieties, troubled romances, and family disputes. Although he recalled her probable futures as being mostly cloudy, Miles had not worried about this because his visions were often unclear and shifting in nature—clarity was not a given. Now darker harbingers gathered around the girl, each one fighting for prominence and shaded with predatory undertones.

Miles shuddered. He felt a protective affection for the girl as a parent might have for a favored and awkward child. Despite her good nature, he had sensed loneliness within, which transcended all her possible lives.

"Miles?" Stephanie said with a wave. "Our assignment?"

"Yes, the plan," Miles stammered. He flipped through his notebook for Klusmeyer's instructions. "The plan, the plan," he said, forcing a smile. "Well, Stephanie, it appears you have a pop quiz on chapter three of Steinbeck's *The Red Pony*. Ah, one of my favorite Steinbeck works."

The students groaned.

"How about a movie instead?" Leo Mazano asked.

Miles turned to the thin, dark-haired boy sitting in the second row by the windows. The morning light slipping through the half-drawn shades illuminated the boy's dull, grey eyes. The beast in Miles' gut dug deeper. He saw needle tracks along the boy's thin arms, and Mazano lying prone and alone on a worn and filthy bed. He saw a father, a man buried in anger, wielding a belt on the cowering boy. He saw the boy handcuffed and led away by police.

"Jesus," Miles uttered. Must all their lives be consumed with hopelessness? What have they done to incur the wrath of all the universes?

"Yes, a movie," Stephanie said. "A Pixar."

Miles shook his head. "A movie? No, not today. I'm sorry. We must complete our assigned tasks. Test conditions, please. Books on the floor and no cell phones. I trust you've kept them in your locker."

"Oh, Miles," Stephanie said. "You're breaking our hearts."

And you, mine, Miles thought.

*

During his lunch break, Miles sought refuge in the library, finding an empty cubbyhole buried behind the periodicals, hidden by the lonely shelves of science and geographic magazines. Whispers hung in the air; their masters unseen. Even in the empty spaces free of children—and the kids were just children, knowing nothing of all the worlds and desires the universes held—probabilities haunted him.

He opened his book and read. He hoped seeking sanctuary in the familiar comfort of his favorite writers would drown out the din, and he'd find shelter in the arcs of imagined lives.

He scanned the pages, but nothing emerged. The letters did not form words. They were only patterns—forms without thought, without story.

He set aside the book.

The voices grew louder. Miles grimaced. He knew the speakers. He knew the kids. They screamed. They pleaded. They cowered under blades of angry indifference.

Stop. Please.

"Miles, what's wrong?"

Miles lifted his head, twisting toward the voice off to his right. It was Stephanie. He felt a thickness gather in his throat. He forced the words to form. "I'm not feeling well, Stephanie. Nothing more."

Stephanie glanced to her left and right and leaned close. "You've been crying," she said, each word carrying the weight of empathy.

"Old men get sad," Miles said. "Please don't tell. I wouldn't want to lose my reputation—you know, the biggest badass substitute in Bismarck."

Stephanie laughed. She also cried. She raged. Probability waves blinked in and out as if a line of Stephanie's was auditioning for parts in a play where every character's arc ended in tragedy.

Miles felt as if he would break down into more tears. He had exposed too much already. The girl needed help, but he could not bear to bring himself to listen or watch. Ashamed of his weakness, Miles stood. "I must go, Stephanie. Sorry." He left without turning. No, he fled.

*

Students jammed the hallways as they left the cafeteria for their afternoon classes. Head down, with his workbag slung over his shoulder, Miles slipped through the torrent of kids. Students called out his name, but he neither stopped nor waved. The voices of those seen and unseen rose, built to a crescendo. Where can I find peace? Miles pleaded to himself as he approached his classroom. Stopping at the door, he considered leaving. At home, locked away in his den, he'd be safe. He could shut out all the worlds, or at least try.

But he didn't leave. He never shirked a responsibility. His wife loved that about him. I am a stand-up guy, he thought bitterly. I always do what's right. What a fool…

He entered the classroom.

*

Stephanie stood in front of his desk, looking distant and small. "Miles, please don't run away from me. You once told us we could tell you anything. You were talking to the whole class, but I knew you meant me."

He couldn't recall the conversation, but that didn't mean it hadn't occurred. Lately he had problems separating the probable lives with the one being led. "You're right. I shouldn't have run away from you. Sorry."

Miles closed the door and checked the clock: Class would begin in fifteen minutes, then the kids would file in and the probability waves would renew their assault. He remembered when he had loved his gift, when he had embraced all the possibilities the worlds offered. He had reveled in the richness of existence and felt privileged to know its secrets. Now all he saw was the cruel and bitter world, no, worlds, humanity, and these kids, had to suffer through. Christ, he loved them. He didn't do this job for the money, not anymore. He did it because he cared for the kids, for the hope they held, blissfully unfazed in their hearts by all the brutality of existence.

Stephanie slipped to the floor. Her backpack landed with a sad thump. Her hair fell over her face and she shook and choked out soft sobs.

Miles rushed to her. He knelt close. "Stephanie, what's going on?"

She turned away and said softly, "I guess young girls get sad, too."

"Yes, and they lead secret lives, fiercely hiding them from all those who care about them," said Miles.

Stephanie nodded. She gathered a breath and spoke. Her words showered him like a meteor storm: all she had endured at the hands of her stepfather—the hopelessness, the degradation, and now the suicidal thoughts. She had carried the secret for years; it was her burden to carry, and to hide.

How had I missed this? Miles lamented. What use is this gift if I can't see the reality in front of me?

Miles studied the girl.

She looked ready to fold in on herself, collapsing under the weight of her sadness. She saw only one future, one terrible end.

Miles smiled.

He understood his gift.

Finally.

He gently pulled on Stephanie's sleeve, guiding her up. "Come with me," he said. "Let's talk. I know you only see one outcome, one way out, but there are other possibilities. Trust me. You may not see them, but I do."

Maranda on Fire
Steve Nelson

I started firewalking after seeing a picture of a monk burn himself to death, but of course it's more complicated than that. Another monk came in to history class where we were studying Vietnam, talking about what a mistake it had been, and about the protests against the war in our country and over there, where they took it a lot more seriously. You see, in Vietnam they're Buddhist, and they've got monks, and to make their point these monks didn't carry signs or pass out flowers. Instead, they'd go to busy city streets, douse themselves with gasoline, light themselves on fire, then just kneel down and burn, not moving a muscle, not flinching, or even gritting their teeth. They'd just burn and melt and die.

In class we were looking up at a slide of one of these monks in flames. Maranda was in class with me, sitting across the darkened room, and I glanced over to see the side of her face catching the light from the screen. Her eyes were fixed ahead like the others and then she asked, "How did he do it? Not feel any pain?" Our teacher said it had something to do with meditation, detachment, letting go, some kind of crazy Buddhist trick he didn't quite understand. The room was quiet for a few more moments, then somebody mumbled something about paper cuts, another mentioned toothaches, and most everyone agreed that this guy was not like us, not even close. But I knew they were saying that

21

because they didn't understand. And though I didn't understand either, how he did it, I knew we weren't that much different from each other, me and that monk. It was just that he'd figured it out, how to control his thoughts, shut off his mind.

That night I was sitting in my friend JD's basement playing poker. It was about ten o'clock. I had a pair of jacks and was wondering if it was good enough to win the $4 pot. Then I realized I didn't care either way. I folded, then at the end of the hand got up and said I was leaving.

"What?" JD asked. "Why?"

"I just don't see the point in it."

"Come on Owen," he said. "We're having fun, hanging out. There doesn't have to be a point, does there?"

"Maybe not, but I just..."

"Is it Maranda?"

"What do you mean, is it Maranda?"

"Something happening with you two?"

"Come on," I said. "Maranda and me have been friends since first grade."

"You've been acting funny around each other lately," he said.

"They haven't even been talking to each other," my other friend Pete added, and I looked at the both of them incredulously, as though they were confusing me with someone else, though really I couldn't believe they'd noticed, that they'd been paying attention at all.

"I'm just tired of playing cards, that's all," I said and left.

On my way home I walked past Maranda's house. She lived on the same block as me; our big backyards touched at the corner. I saw the light on in her bedroom and slowed, but didn't see her. We'd been friends, like I said, for a long time. She'd never been a tomboy exactly but had always liked to play kickball, soccer, Ghost in the Graveyard. That was our favorite. Base was the cedar deck on the back of her house and there were lots of good hiding spots in the evergreens that ran between our yards. Some days if it was just the two of us we'd race back and forth from one end of her yard to the other. Maranda was faster than me when we were kids and usually won, but neither of us cared. It was just fun to race.

We weren't quite kids anymore though. That had all changed the last weekend of summer. Maranda had been gone July and most of August to her aunt's farm in Gettysburg, where she went every year. When she returned, I didn't recognize her. I was at a party and I saw her profile from across the room and I said, "Wow, who is that?" When she turned and smiled at me I realized it was Maranda, but she looked taller, thinner, with her cheek bones higher on her face. Her skin had a new glow to it, and she'd let her hair go long. It was down to her shoulders and lighter than its usual brownish red. She walked up to me smiling and gave me a hug, which was something new. As she held me, I felt her breasts on me, and this was new too. "Owen," she said finally. "How are you?" Even the sound of my name coming from her mouth was different. This was a new Maranda.

The party was at Ginny Bauer's place, which was an old farmhouse with a big barn, silo, and a few acres of property. Most of the houses in our town were built in the '50s and '60s, so when you went to Ginny's, you really felt like you were going somewhere, doing something different, and because her parents liked to travel she had a lot of parties. This night just about everyone was there, and there was lots of beer, which I was drinking, and rum punch, which Maranda was drinking. Neither of us had ever done much drinking, and we began to feel pretty carefree in a short while.

It was a warm night. The house had a big in-ground pool, and most were hanging out there, doing cannonballs or complaining about being splashed, but Maranda and I found ourselves stealing away, walking back behind the barn where we sat on some old tractor tires and unexpectedly began to kiss. At first I couldn't believe it was me and Maranda, but she was so warm and curvy, such a good kisser, that after a few moments I forgot about that. And as we kept on I forgot about everything else. I'd kissed girls before, but only awkwardly. This was different: it was like the rest of the world had disappeared, and I think I really lost track of myself for the first time in my life.

But I guess you can only kiss for so long, or maybe Maranda had drunk more than I. After a while she stopped kissing me and was unbuttoning me and all of sudden she'd taken us beyond just kissing, and I guess I'd been dreaming about something like this happening. Of course I had daydreams, night dreams, all kinds of dreams—but I hadn't expected them to ever come true. I was awash in sensation; this tingling feeling was shooting all the way to my fingers and toes. At the same time the world had come back to me, and I opened my eyes, was looking around, trying to get my bearings, checking to be sure no one was watching, and then I guess I couldn't resist looking down at Maranda, and she was pulling her hair back from her face, and like I said this new profile of hers was absolutely beautiful, and I felt myself smile at the sight of us.

But I guess she must've felt me looking at her because she opened her eyes and looked up at me, and from straight on she looked like the old Maranda, the old friend I'd played with all my life. She must have seen something too, maybe the same thing, because she pulled herself back quickly as if startled. Then we both looked away from each other. She got up and stepped away while I stood and buttoned up. She'd pointed herself away from me and I felt myself wanting to say something, but only let out a low "Uhhmmm..." She began to walk quickly back to the party with her long, loping stride, and I followed behind.

We'd avoided each other since then—not so much as looking each other in the eye—and I'd been doing all I could to stop thinking about her. But it was hard because I didn't know exactly *what* I was thinking. I only knew that I didn't feel like myself when I thought about her, and that I'd wake each morning before five o'clock feeling that all the air had been sucked out of me. I'd try to fall back to sleep, but never could, feeling at turns dirty, raw, weepy, weak, or desperate. This anguish was something I'd never really experienced before in my life as everything had always gone along just well enough. Me and my friends, who I'd always done most everything with, didn't do sports or drugs, and we didn't have girlfriends. I'd been getting tired of that. I had hoped it might change that year and that something might actually matter, but then finally something of consequence did happen and it only made everything worse.

When I got home that night my parents were out, gone as every Friday during the season to my brother's football game. Our town was mad for football, and my brother was the team's starting center. He said it was one of the most important positions on the team, but I figured who'd want to be the center—having the quarterback putting his hands between your legs every play? Sometimes he wanted to practice snapping the ball to me, but after the first time I always came up with a good excuse to avoid it, and he'd get our dad to do it instead. I guess I didn't understand football, or my brother, or my parents that well. But this had never been a big problem for me. It's not like I thought I'd be better off with another family. My mom with her television shows and coupons, my dad with his job and newspaper, my brother always hiking his football, they were my family. I couldn't imagine things any other way. It just so happened that I was the one always on the outside. Sometimes I even felt like a visitor, like I was watching them be a family. But this was just the way things had always been. I was used to it.

I went to my room and started looking through some boxes of old papers and pictures and stuff. I knew I was too young to be sitting home on a Friday night reminiscing, but there I was looking over old class pictures from grade school and wondering where the years had gone. And there were other pictures too—a big group of us eating popsicles on Maranda's back deck on the Fourth of July; Maranda and I at Six Flags, smiling at the camera, not a care in the world. I wondered again how it had happened. There'd been no reason for us to wander off together, go sit on tires, kiss, any of it. We'd even talked about it over the years when others had coupled up. We could see how silly it was—the hand-holding, phone calls, dates, the inevitable break-ups. "Just gets in the way," we'd agreed, though exactly what it got in the way of we didn't say. I thought maybe we'd talked about others as a way of talking about ourselves, but it had never felt like that. It had just felt like, well, Maranda and I, like it always had. I shook my head and told myself I had to stop thinking about her. But I knew it wasn't as simple as telling myself to stop. I had to keep my mind occupied.

I put the pictures away and went through some of my old schoolwork, finally pulling out a report I'd done on firewalking in junior high. According to my report, firewalking had been used as a ritual by lots of different cultures, as an initiation into manhood, proof of faith or bravery, or an act of penance. And even though the fire would be between 600 and 1200 degrees, the key was simply telling yourself you wouldn't get burned. You had to be "in the moment" and unafraid, which isn't easy because we're born with two fears—of falling and of fire.

I thought about that and the fact that we acquired all our other fears over time through living. It seemed to me that fear of falling and fear of fire were both kind of the same thing—fear of death. I figured that's what all fears were based on and thought that would have been an interesting angle to add to my report, though of course I hadn't been thinking about that in junior high. I stopped and tried to remember what I had been thinking about then, what had kept my mind occupied, but I couldn't recall. Then I thought back to that monk we'd seen burning up in history class that day, and that's when I decided maybe I should try, not burn or kill myself, but firewalking. I needed to do something and thought if I could walk on fire I'd kind of be like that monk—at least I'd have more control over things.

In our town you could burn your leaves, so the next Friday night, after my parents had gone to the game, I raked the leaves from the back yard into a ten-by-three-foot section behind the garage. I covered them over with small pieces of kindling and mulch we got for free from the city dump, then doused it all with lighter fluid, threw down a match, and watched the fire burn. I couldn't walk over it until the flames had died down and there were only coals—the embers. While waiting I tried to sit and relax, not meditating exactly (I didn't know what that was) but just sitting there close to the fire, watching the flames dance, feeling the heat, listening to the the crackles and hiss. All week I'd been thinking about it, preparing myself, imagining myself walking over the coals. Now I was going to do it.

I had set up a small tube of water at the end of the run, just in case. After the flames died down, I got up and walked around the edge of the bed barefoot, figuring I would build up to it gradually, like settling down into a steaming hot bath. I did this a few times, concentrating not on my feet or the fire but my breathing like I was supposed to. Finally I told myself it was time to go through. I stood at the edge, and standing close like that, in my bare feet, it was easy to stay "in the moment" because all my senses were paying close attention. It was survival instinct, I suppose, like peering over the edge of a cliff. I stood a few moments, took some deep breaths, looked ahead, exhaled one more time slowly, then took a step, then another, then a third. The coals felt crunchy like eggshells. I could feel that, but not any heat, not any pain, and I felt myself smile at this realization. Then I felt it—sharp prickles of heat under me—and I lunged forward, getting off the coals in two quick strides. I stepped into the tub of water swearing quietly, but when I stepped out a minute later I couldn't feel any pain. Back in the house I inspected my feet and saw there were no blisters or burn marks. I rubbed a little aloe vera on them just to be safe, then told myself though I hadn't made it all the way, it was a start, I'd walked on fire, and more importantly, I'd been "in the moment," had "let go," and stopped thinking about Maranda. Of course, once I told myself this, I started thinking about her again. But still it was progress. And it was nice to have gotten away from my thoughts for a while.

The next Friday night I set up another fire. As it got going, I strolled around the perimeter again, breathing in and out, visualizing myself going through. When it was time to walk it I did so without a thought, not feeling the fire at all, not even realizing I was moving until I was done and stepping back onto the grass. When I looked back over the fire bed I could hardly believe I'd just gone through it. I had no recollection. My feet felt fine. I waited a few minutes, then did it again. Same result. I did it again. Success.

"What are you doing?" a voice asked from behind me. I looked over. It was Maranda.

I was sure she'd seen me so there was no sense in denying it. "Firewalking," I said.

"Why?" she asked calmly.

"Something to do, I guess."

"Can I try?" she asked, coming closer.

"I don't know," I told her. "You've got to plan for it. You've got to think about it. You can't just jump on and—"

"I'm going to try," she said, taking off her shoes.

"I don't know, Maranda."

"You just did it, right?"

"Yeah," I said, and she looked straight at me and shrugged. This is how she'd always been. If I or someone else could do something, climb a tree, go off the high dive, bike around the block in under two minutes, she could do it too. Or at least she'd try. So I didn't argue with her but just watched as she stood on the edge of the fire and took a few deep breaths. "Just breathe," I said. "And don't look at it."

She gazed ahead, which gave me an opportunity to really look at her, and again I was amazed that this was Maranda, so regal and lovely and curvy. She was wearing a snug white sweater and blue jeans, which she'd pulled up around her calves. She exhaled once hard, then took a step forward, then another. I walked backwards to the end of the fire and looking at her face almost straight on I could see again that she wasn't as beautiful as from the side; her eyes were a little too close together, her chin a little square, that there was still some of that obtuse matter-of-fact quality in her that had always surfaced when she was concentrating. She looked like the old Maranda again as she was making steady progress across the embers towards me. As soon as she'd finished and set her feet onto the grass beside me, she relaxed and smiled, and I was nearly knocked over by her transformation back to a beauty.

"Wow," I said.

"I did it," she said excitedly.

"Yeah."

When she turned to go past me I could smell the shampoo in her hair. She went to pick up her shoes, turned halfway towards me, then said, "You know that party?"

"Yeah," I said quickly.

"I don't know what happened."

"Me either," I said. "That was...strange."

"I never, I mean, I never did that before," she told me. "I don't want you to think that I—"

"No," I said. "Of course not. I didn't think that. I just...well, I guess I don't know."

"We can just forget about it, right?"

"Yeah, we should. I mean, well, maybe..."

"You don't want to forget about it?" she asked, turning towards me.

"I don't know," I said, looking down.

I could sense she was waiting for me to say something more to her, but nothing came to mind. "Well, I think we should just forget about it," she said, then turned and walked back towards her house.

After she left I realized I'd been spending my energy trying to stop thinking about Maranda and what had happened, but hadn't considered what she'd been thinking or feeling. And I began to think about that, especially what she was thinking about me, and that was even worse. I didn't feel just empty, but nauseous. I tried to walk the fire again that night, but I took one step and my feet were burning. Concentrate, I told myself. Then I said, no, don't concentrate. And then I gave up; I knew I was trying too hard.

During the week I tried to do other things to keep my mind busy. One day I went to the basement and tried to work out with my brother's weight set. Another day I went for a long walk to the park at the other end of town. I worked on some old card tricks I used to be able to do pretty well. One night I snuck two beers from the basement fridge and drank them while I played chess on my computer. But nothing worked. When I'd see Maranda in school I couldn't help but watch her, but she never looked my way. When my eyes were on her I'd get those tingling sensations, but I could hardly enjoy them because as soon as I looked away it was like I was catching myself, and then I'd feel lost, adrift like a kid left behind at the mall.

Finally Friday came and I could do my firewalking again. And Maranda came over again too, and we took turns walking the fire, not talking much in between, and when we did, it was just about the fire, or school, or something else unimportant. We didn't talk about each other, or that night. We weren't comfortable like we'd been before, but when I was with her I didn't feel quite so beat up about things—everything in me just sort of quieted down. Still, we didn't look each other in the eye, even when we said goodnight and she went through the evergreens towards her house. After she left and I put out the fire, I tried to get to sleep as soon possible because I knew if I waited too long, the swirling would come back.

Somehow news of our firewalking got out and the next Friday night there was a small crowd of kids from school gathered in my back yard watching me set up. A few said they wanted to try, but most just wanted to watch. I'd never had much attention paid to me, so this was something new, and I kind of liked it, those dozen or so people watching me get the fire going, asking questions, waiting to see me walk it. JD and Pete were there and they were looking at me like they didn't know me. "You should try it," I said to them, but they just shook their heads.

Maranda came over just after I'd finished my first pass and she said, "What's going on?" to no one in particular, and they filled her in, as if she had no previous knowledge of the firewalking, and she let them believe that was the case.

After I'd gone, two guys who'd been suspended from the football team tried, but neither could make it more than two steps without yowling and jumping off. Then a guy from the soccer team tried and he made it across, but nearly ran doing so, and not surprisingly burned the balls of his feet. A couple of girls consoled him while a guy named Rob, who'd been a kid with us all along but who'd been sent away to juvenile detention facility that summer for winning a fight a little too decisively, tried next. He moved across the coals gingerly, methodically, breathing loudly through gritted teeth, but he made it all the way across. When he was done he got high-fives from the other guys and said it was just a matter of "tuning things out." But I could see when he pulled his socks and shoes on that his feet were hurting a bit. I did another pass then someone got a call on their cell phone about a party starting up and everyone split and it was just Maranda and I.

"Why didn't you walk?" I asked her.

She just shrugged and bent to take off her shoes. "I'll go now."

Because I'd run out of leaves to burn, and maybe because there'd been a crowd, I'd added extra wood chips and the fire was hotter than ever before. Though Maranda walked it without getting hurt, she said she'd felt it a little, the heat on her skin, and told me to be careful when I said I was going to go one more time.

I stood at the edge of the fire, looked down at it, then up at the night sky. The branches of the empty trees swayed in the wind. I took in a deep breath and even with the fire before me, I could smell October in the air, feel the chill of autumn coming, and then I almost laughed at the ridiculousness of it, walking on fire in my back yard. It was as if this was the first time I realized what I was doing, as opposed to just being bent on doing it, and I felt glad, like something had been lifted off of me.

I looked over at Maranda. She was looking at me, and I felt myself smile at her. I looked ahead then, took a few deep breaths, and stepped forward. I took two, three steps and felt nothing. I was even able to tell myself I was feeling nothing, and still to keep on. I took another step, then another, into the middle of the fire, the hottest stretch of it, then I felt myself coming to a stop and I began counting: one...two...three...four....

While before, when I'd walked the fire successfully, I'd had no clear thoughts, just a blank mind, had shut it off, this time I was still aware of myself, and had even a dim recognition of the fire hissing below me. But I felt no pain, felt nothing, and just stood motionless counting...five...six...seven....

I got all the way up to ten then felt something—Maranda's hand grabbing mine. Then I felt myself grabbing back. And then the pain came rushing to me, the feeling of my feet getting seared, as if the skin was being peeled off.

I jumped sideways towards Maranda and we got twisted around each other and fell onto the edge of the fire, her shoulder dipping into the coals, the ends of her hair getting singed. She let out a little scream as we scrambled together onto the grass. And then we just lay there, wrapped around each other. I had my eyes closed, then opened them to see Maranda looking straight at me.

"Are you okay?" she asked.

"Hurts a little," I said.

"Me too," she told me. She was looking right at me, and I realized she was beautiful, even straight on like this.

"But this feels good," I told her and pulled her closer to me.

She sighed and pressed her head into my neck and shoulder. "Me too," she said. "I feel good." And we stayed there a few more minutes until finally she put her mouth to my ear and said, "Let's go to my house."

"Okay," I said and we got up and picked up our shoes. My feet stung a bit, but it was bearable, and Maranda and I put our arms around each other and went through the evergreens towards her house.

When she let out another sigh, I kissed the top of her head and pulled her closer to me. Maranda, I thought. Maranda. I didn't want to stop thinking about her after all.

Change the rules...

"a wonderfully wide world awaited her"

Jenny Can't Go Back to Bismarck

Bozeman Before the Fire
Frank T. Sikora

Part One

Although I had been aware of Emma, the cruel, intriguing, and terribly lonely White Witch of Empathy, for a number of years, I first spoke to the girl in 1963 at the Bozeman Founder's Day picnic. Held annually at Centennial Park on the last weekend of August, the picnic offered a final chance for families to gather for an afternoon of games, food, and drink before summer ended, one last time for the local kids to inhale the breath of summer before school started.

I loved the old park. It sat on the western edge of town, nestled in a lush, green basin at more than 4,800 feet above sea level. Surrounded by the rugged and forested Tobacco Mountains to the west and the taller, snowcapped Gallatin Mountains to the south, the park lay in an area known as the Valley of Flowers. On that day, the weather was ideal for picnicking, a comfortable 81 degrees with a light, cooling breeze drifting in from the north.

Besides Emma, a dozen other children and young adults from the Oncology Ward of Deaconess Memorial Hospital attended the picnic. This was not unusual. Every year the hospital dragged its young patients out into the sun and into full view of the town's more fortunate families. A cynic might have considered the hospital's action nothing more than a publicity stunt—an opportunity to gather sympathy and to acquire new donors for its annual fundraising drive. I thought it was a good idea for the sick kids to play with the healthy children. For one afternoon they could feel normal. They could feel the wind at their backs and the warmth of natural light on their shoulders.

The sick children were easy to spot. They were the ones swaddled in sweatshirts, sweatpants, and gloves. They were all achingly thin, with dark eyes, and, of course, bald, which the boys hid with baseball hats donated by the University of Montana Sports Department. The girls wore colorful scarves and displayed them with fashionable pride. Emma wore neither; although, she did have a sun hat, which I assumed her nurse had given her to protect her head. Yet, during the short time I had watched Emma, she had yet to wear it. She also refused to wear traditional clothing; instead, she wore her hospital pajamas, robe, and slippers as if she was telling the world, "Yes, I'm sick. I'm ugly. If you don't like what you see, then look away."

I assumed she hadn't noticed me when I approached her. I had kept myself hidden walking along the grey, star-soaked, probability corridors of the Spaces-in-Between—my home and the home for my fellow wizards, the so-called, "Agents of Manipulation." It is in here, in the Spaces-in-Between, the gray, lightless corridors intertwined between the mortal world of light and death and the gifted world of probability and darkness that the decisions that affect the course of human events are made.

I took residence in the Spaces-in-Between ten years ago after my death at the age of eighty-five. I will exist here for another fifty or sixty years, retaining during these "gifted years" the semblance of flesh and blood and the curse of memory and emotion. Then, like all mortal creatures, I'll expire.

I missed the world of light and its simple pleasures, such as the taste of a good meal, the touch of a friend, or a walk in the mountains, but I did not come to reconnect with my past. I came to get a closer look at this unusual young White Witch, and, perhaps, to understand the motivations behind her aberrant behavior.

Emma sat alone on a picnic blanket at the bottom of a small hill, ignoring a gentle game of badminton going on about forty feet behind her. The participants were a mixture of healthy and sick children, the latter watched closely by their nurses and parents from the picnic tables at the top of the hill.

During my first half hour of observation, I watched Emma cast an all-purpose protection spell over the children attending the picnic and a general healing spell on one of the healthy children, a stocky, red-haired boy of ten, which she expertly delivered in a clear, strong voice that both completed the job but avoided drawing attention.

It wasn't apparent to me why she had focused on this young boy. Though overweight, he appeared healthy. Perhaps Emma was alarmed by his occasional cough and feared he might develop pneumonia or some other congestive ailment. Most likely, she simply sensed something wrong within him. White Witches are wonderfully perceptive—they must be for the welfare of the children in their stead: their classmates, neighbors, and friends.

Sadly, their gifts are counterbalanced by a cruel susceptibility to cancer and other virulent diseases. With bitter irony, White Witches' healing and protection spells are virtually ineffective on themselves. Most die by their early twenties. Is this fair? No. But I don't make the rules. I abide by them. Besides, as my mentor once said to me, "Fair ends the moment you leave the womb. Sometimes before."

After completing the spells, Emma smiled and sighed; a look of contentment on her ashen face. White Witches experience a spiritual blissfulness when helping others, a small compensation for taking on the ills of the world. The lovely moment, however, passed quickly. With a crushing air of fatigue, she opened her book —a worn, hard copy of *Anna Karenina*, and slowly flipped through its pages.

The girl looked as if she might collapse and die on the spot. Her eyes were a disturbing shade of pale green with gray smudges for pupils. Black veins scorched jagged trails across her pallid cheeks. Gray, flaking skin covered her delicate hands, which looked too brittle to hold her copy of Tolstoy's classic.

I knew her cancer had recently reached Stage IV. In fewer than six months, it had metastasized from both her lungs to her lymph nodes and into her brain. I knew her disease intimately. It was I who had set the disease on its ravenous course.

As I moved in closer to Emma, I heard a cavernous echo within her chest. Each breath, I thought, must feel like a knife shearing through her lungs, each step just one in a long, arduous forced march. Though only fourteen years old, she looked like an exhausted fifty.

Looking down at this living carcass, I almost felt sorry for the little White Witch.

After a few silent minutes, she began speaking in a soft, barely audible voice. It was unclear whether she was reciting from her book or engaged in a conversation with herself, which in itself would not have been unusual. White Witches tend to be solitary creatures with few friends. At first, the words were indecipherable with the accents seemingly placed on the wrong syllables. Then, after another minute or two had passed, I recognized the language; it was an obscure and long-dead Gaelic dialect, and then I recognized the content. It was a prayer, a prayer of forgiveness, one my mother had taught me as a child, one I had buried deep within the forgotten corridors of my memory. It was a prayer for the slaughtered, the untold, and uncounted that have perished at the hands of the powerful and the indifferent.

Impressive, I thought, and disconcerting. Her prayer confirmed my suspicions that she had indeed looked into my history, perhaps even ventured into my personal corridors, and that her actions—better yet, her inactions—contributed to the death of my grandniece, my sister's only grandchild, Marie, who was also a classmate of Emma's. It was a death Emma could have prevented, and a death, in my mind, that justified my actions.

Last December, while riding the bus to school, Marie had mentioned to a friend that she hadn't been feeling well and that she had awoken that morning feeling nauseous with a horrific headache. Her friend encouraged her to see the nurse, or at least tell one of her teachers. Marie did neither. I suspect she didn't want to miss rehearsals. She had a part in her school's winter production of *The Unsinkable Molly Brown*. Later in the day, she even mentioned to the same friend that she was feeling better, and appeared to be fine during rehearsal and on the bus ride home.

That same night, Marie collapsed shortly after dinner with her family. She had suffered a brain aneurism and died two days later at Deaconess Memorial, three rooms down from where Emma would eventually take residence.

Throughout the whole day, Emma had opportunity after opportunity to intervene. She sat behind Marie on the bus and did nothing. She sat two desks behind Marie in class and did nothing. She engaged in conversation with Marie during passing periods and did nothing. The White Witch of Empathy didn't offer one token healing spell. She stood by and watched. She knew Marie was ill. She let her die, breaking the collective hearts of those who loved the girl, including me.

I had no idea why Emma would behave so abominably. It didn't make sense. She had to have known I would take it personally; that her deplorable actions toward Marie were unacceptable and would draw attention to her. A White Witch always acts in the interest of the other children. Until Emma, the probability of a White Witch behaving in direct contrast to her nature had never even been considered. Many of my associates still can't fathom the possibility.

Even more distressing than Marie's unnecessary death, especially to those above me, was the possibility that Emma had entered the Spaces-in-Between, a dangerous precedent. To quote one of my associates, "This job is hard enough. There are already too many variables. You think the world is screwed up now? The last thing we need is a bunch of angry White Witches meddling in our affairs." Wizards still possess an archaic view of a woman's place in the natural and unnatural order of the world.

I didn't disagree. A wizard's work was difficult, determining probabilities and outcomes based on endless known variables and uncountable unknown variables. Interference could not be tolerated.

Yet, this young witch still intrigued me for a number of reasons, including her remarkable resiliency to her disease and her unprecedented emergence. Her mother was neither a witch herself nor related to any known coven of White Witches: charity, chastity, kindness, forgiveness, sorrow and, of course, the most powerful coven of all—empathy. Her mother was just a hideously ugly, mortal woman of no discernible talent and even lesser morals who only gave up Emma for adoption after failing to sell her on the black market. Her father might have possessed a wizard's genetic lineage, but he died shortly after Emma's birth, the poor bastard spontaneously combusting in the checkout line at the grocery store. Emma was an anomaly, an incalculable and beyond rare statistical improbability. Ordinary women simply did not give birth to White Witches.

Emma continued her incantation another few minutes until she stopped and looked up at the sky. A light breeze blew the remaining thin strands of her hair across her face. She did not brush them away. Instead, she reached over and grabbed her hat and placed it on her head, casting her harsh, angular features in shadow. I expected her to either go back to her book or to her prayers. Rather, she posed a question: "Do you remember Dresden?"

I did not answer. I wasn't sure whom she was speaking to. There weren't any children or adults within listening distance. Unless, I had accidentally slipped out of the Spaces and exposed myself, I should have gone unnoticed.

"Wizard, I repeat, do you remember Dresden?"

Of course I remembered Dresden, Germany. During the Sixth Great Conflict of Man, the war mortals know as World War II, I had done my best to stop the senseless bombing of that beautiful city and failed—one of my bitterest failures. Bombing that beautiful city was not my idea. Stronger Wizards than I had persuaded the Allied Command that it was necessary.

With a bemused sigh, she said, "Wizard, please answer. I know you heard me. I can hear you skulking around like some third-rate aberration. You might as well have approached me wearing a cowbell around your neck."

A White Witch with a sense of humor! Now I knew this girl was special, and yes, despite her cruelty, I found her interesting. Consumed with self-righteousness, most White Witches are a joyless lot, self-important dullards incapable of appreciating a joke much less cracking one. I laughed and emerged from the Spaces-in-Between. "You know me, then," I said. "You know my intentions?"

"Of course. I understand completely. Whom do you think my prayers were for?"

"For me?"

"Why, yes," she said and set aside her book. She rolled back the sleeves of her hospital gown and robe, revealing bandages and dark black bruises, a result from too many needles assaulting her skin. "Why shouldn't I pray for the creature responsible for all this? Hadn't Jesus said to love thine enemy? Why shouldn't I pray for the man who has set out to kill me and my child?"

"You're pregnant?"

Emma flashed that soul-sickening grin—crooked black teeth set amid dead white gums that still haunts me. "Not at this moment, but the last time I peeked into the Spaces-in-Between, that loveless world you call home, where you and your cronies play roulette with the futures of those whom you confess to love, I saw an interesting array of probabilities. It seems I have many possible futures, Wizard—some you haven't even considered, and some you should fear."

Part Two

At this point, I considered murdering the girl outright, forgoing the charade of her illness. I could have burned her right where she sat, reducing the pale, wretchedly thin girl to a teapot high pile of ash and dust. I could also have ripped her heart out of her chest and laid it on her picnic blanket, but these actions might have brought undue attention toward me. Besides, I wasn't a teenage girl governed by impulses. I lived by reason, and I had my own bosses to contend with, and they preferred the results of my work looked like natural causes. So I cradled my temper. Summoning my best fatherly tone, I said, "Emma, it's a lovely day. Perhaps you should spend time with the other children and join in the fun. A little exercise always works wonders."

"Whacking plastic little birdies is not what I consider fun. Besides, I must keep my strength, and you haven't answered my question. Do you remember Dresden?"

"What has Dresden got to do with anything? Is this part of your studies?"

"Just answer, please," she said. "We don't have all day. Some of us aren't in the best of health."

"Yes, yes, I remember Dresden, but I don't like your tone. It suggests or implies that I or my associates share a duplicity in the city's tragic course of events."

With a hard, squinty-eyed scowl and a shrug of disappointment, she said, "Share a duplicity? Is that the course you want our discussion to take? Obfuscation? Deceit? If so, this discussion has arrived dead on the proverbial doorstep." She stopped and brought her hand to her face and picked at a flake of dead skin on her cheek and slowly, deliberately pulled at it as if she were ripping off a bandage. She then placed it on her tongue and ate it. When I didn't respond, she frowned.

"Yes, obfuscation," she said grinning. "I believe that is the correct word. Obfuscation. You must excuse me. My only vanity is my vocabulary, and right now it is not what it should be. I've missed the last three months of the school year, and I'm not always at my best with my current tutor. You know, with the cancer rotting away my brain and all."

"Your vocabulary is more than sufficient, Emma. Please get to your point."

"What's the hurry? You have all the time in the world. I'm the one who is under your dangling sword."

"An inappropriate metaphor, Emma. Rude and untrue."

She offered an arrogant shrug. "Very well. If you insist, I will accommodate your charade." She paused for a moment and glanced back at the kids playing. "How are things back home? What's it like hanging out with nothing but feeble old farts, spending your last short years bitching and moaning about the new breed of wizards, the lack of standards, plans gone awry, worlds gone to shit, and women you should have fucked, or worse, shouldn't have?"

"Your vulgarity surprises me, Emma. I expect more from a White Witch, especially an empathetic one."

"Oh, don't look so surprised. You should know there is nothing I could say or do that would surprise you." She laughed, a hideous cackle that drew the attention of the children playing. They stopped and stared briefly at her, probably wondering if it was her time. Emma paid them no attention. "Come, sit, old man," she said. "You look tired. Shall we continue our discussion?"

I never liked taking orders, especially from those beneath me, but I had come to gather information, to understand the beast slouching within this unique young witch—the monstrosity that murdered my grandniece. I did not want to engage with this young girl. I would rather have continued my observations and actions from afar, without engagement, and to treat her as just another variable to determine and exercise, but the chance had passed. I could not escape her detection. So, I sat.

"Thank you, Nathan," she said softly, offering a broad, maybe even genuine smile. "Despite all your flaws, your manners remain impeccable."

I tried to suppress my own smile, but failed. I must confess that the girl did have a certain charisma.

Emma folded her hands across her lap. "Now, about Dresden. Tell me your thoughts. What do you think happened?"

"Why do you care what I think? I suspect you don't give two hoots about my opinion. You're simply itching to give me yours."

"Oh, Nathan," she said amid another arrogant shrug. The dying girl possessed a confidence born of arrogance and delusion. "That is your name, right? Nathan Dreary, former printer from Milwaukee. After you retired, you moved to Bozeman, but you didn't choose to live with your sister. Instead, you chose to live among the grizzly bears and bobcats of the Gallatin National Forest in a quaint three-room cabin in the mountains. Just you, alone, until heart failure forced you into the dreaded and oh-so-off-limits corridors of probability, home of the not-so-all-knowing and the not-so-all-powerful, soon-to-be-obsolete boys club—lackeys to creatures too frightened to show themselves, and so scared that they sent their errand boy to finally confront me. Am I right, Mr. Dreary?"

"Yes, Emma. Your research is both accurate and delusional," I said. "You've drawn our attention, but I suggest you don't make the mistake of over estimating your importance or underestimating our resolve."

"I will do my best," she said with a dismissive wave. "But, enough about me. Before we continue, let's talk about you. Tell me, Nathan. Why the life alone? No wife? And from what I have gathered there wasn't even one girlfriend during all your eighty odd years. Why? Were you impotent? Did you prefer slender young boys, all white, sleek, and wet?"

"Don't push me, Witch. Even my patience has limits. Get on with your lecture."

"You're right. I must keep moving. If we linger too long, my nurse will get suspicious. My adoptive parents will worry. They will think you've come here to seduce and sodomize me."

I chose not to respond to the girl's taunt because as I stared into the withered young girl's eyes, I saw fear. Despite her bravado, her gifts, and her psychotic determination, she understood that she could not win her battle with her disease, or with me, or with the powers that had developed an interest in this girl. I waited for her to continue.

"Very well, Nathan, let me give you a history lesson, one I suspect you may already know, but humor me as I will humor you, okay? Good."

The White Witch leaned forward as if telling me a secret. Her dull, grey eyes had finally shown a modicum of light. "It was in the winter of 1945, near the end of the war, a war whose ending was very much a *fait accompli*, a probability wave that could not be quartered. The Allies were going to win. The Russians were going to invade, pillage, and rape the skeletal remains of the German Empire, and yet the British and Americans decided to launch a massive air assault on the German city of Dresden, their combined forces dropping thousands of tons of highly explosive bombs and incendiary devices on the city, creating a massive firestorm that killed more than 35,000 people. Some say it was more like 100,000, but people like to exaggerate, like 35,000 broiled and asphyxiated Germans wasn't enough to constitute a tragedy. People like big numbers. You like numbers, too. Hell, I like numbers. Without them, we're just primates speaking in tongues." She paused and inhaled a long, hard-earned breath. "Are you still with me?"

"Yes, believe it or not, I'm keeping up."

"Good. I'm not always sure my points are clear. I do ramble. You know—"

"Yes, the cancer. It's bad. Please, get on with this."

The White Witch chuckled. "Now, I know what you're thinking. Who cares whether a handful of Germans died? Didn't the civilian population deserve their fate? By their silence and inaction, they supported Hitler and his minions and thus were responsible for the deaths of more than 80 million souls, including 6 million Jews. My question for you, Nathan, is—"

I raised my hands. "Emma, do not imply that I or any of my colleagues were behind the start of this war, much less the Holocaust. This was a war of men. You know yourself, a Witch or a Wizard's powers are limited. You can't save everyone, nor can I persuade the hardest of men or Wizard to accommodate reason."

Emma rolled her eyes and held out her arms as if to embrace the world. With a vile smile, she said, "There's no need to lie to me, Nathan. There's no need to argue with me. I know you don't pull the strings behind this great and secret show; it's much worse. You are the string, the delusional string. Whether it is man or witch, you believe you have control over me and all the other little marionettes you frivolously command. You bathe in this control. It cleanses you of your cowardice. You shiver like a frightened dog before your cruel masters, licking their hands to avoid the whip."

The poor girl was right. I should have known better and not argued. Arguing with crazy is a futile endeavor.

"Now you're pouting? Lord, Nathan, you're a sensitive fellow. Please, stay focused. My question is simple: Why did the Allies attack Dresden? It held little military significance or strategic value. No, don't answer. Let me continue. I'm enjoying our little conversation."

"Right now it's more rant than conversation."

"True, true," she agreed, adding another smarmy shrug, this one more self-important than the previous ones.

"Nathan, I do appreciate your patience. No one pays any real attention to me; no one indulges me like you. The nurses stick me with their needles and scamper away. My doctors huddle over me amazed that I'm still alive. Sometimes I hear them whispering in the hall like seventh grade boys comparing erections. It is during these times I wish I knew my birth mother. Mom means well, but since my illness she has become distant. In her heart, she has already buried me."

"You don't want to know her," I said. "Your birth mother was one step above a common prostitute, sleeping with an indiscriminate number of men for a bed and a meal."

"I suspected, but still," she replied, "I must admit there are times I feel less than adequate. I often wondered if she was pretty. Silly, given that I am not."

I thought I might have seen a tear, but it might have been the strain of conversation. The girl was not well. "Emma, I am begging you. Please, get to the point."

Emma opened her mouth to speak, but then just lowered her head and looked as if all her energy had been spent—as if a breeze might blow her away like dandelion dust. I reached out to her. "Emma?"

She pushed my hand away. "I'm okay. I don't want your sympathy. I detest the irony."

I was not without compassion. White Witches are not our enemies; they serve the world as designed and then expire, as they have for thousands upon thousands of years. Yes, they suffer. Rarely are they loved. They are terrifically ugly, and Emma was not an exception, probably even more so than most. Even before her chemotherapy and radiation treatments, Emma's skin was pockmarked with long-term acne and dark red scars. Her obscenely exaggerated features looked as if she were carved out of sharp stone. "Emma, Dresden?"

"I'm sorry," Emma said wearily. She took a long breath, exhaled, and continued. "The Allies' position, that they could weaken the resolve of the enemy by inflicting mass civilian casualties, was nothing more than a self-serving façade, another whopper of a lie. They tried to convince the world that bombing the German people down to their last collective breaths would motivate the German command to capitulate. Their theory was unsubstantiated by history and by the present. The German command did not give a rat fuck about its people. The German leaders loved their people as a carpenter loved his tools—useful objects that were easily discarded when obsolete or worn. I'm sure you see the irony."

"Yes, yes," I said. "I'm not as dense as you think."

Emma looked back at the children, who had ceased their game and were walking back up the hill. She watched until they all made it back to the main tent. Turning back to face me, she said, "Nathan, as you have probably surmised, I've been to your home in the Spaces-in-Between."

I nodded.

"Yes, I've been a bad girl. Many times. I've watched you as you slept. I've watched you scheme with your cronies, huddling together in your putrid little hovels. Mercy, what forces bind you to such shameful and squalid conditions?"

I didn't reply.

"Nathan, I hope you will forgive my intrusions. I know it's unsettling, but I want you to remember that I know your heart. I've eavesdropped on your conversations. I've listened to you and your sad ilk talk about your grandchildren and how much they mean to you, how much you love them, and how much you resent not being able to see them once you have permanently moved into the Spaces." She smiled coyly. "I guess not all wizards live lives of frustration."

I stood. I had grown tired of her insults, each all-too-achingly true.

She reached out her hand and grabbed mine. "Nathan, I've even watched your dreams. Yes, your dreams. Honestly, I didn't think you were still capable of dreaming. Guilt haunts you. You suffer for Dresden and every decision of neglect and incompetence. You know, as well as I, that the age of Wizards is near its end, and I not only applaud its demise, I shall hasten it." She paused. "Dreaming. I suspect it is your only respite from all that you have endured. Despite all your powers, you're a sad lot. I never thought that the gods could be so incredibly lonely."

I searched for words. I searched for clarity. I was appalled at her indiscretions, her intrusions, and her conclusion. All I could stammer out was a pathetic, "It's not so bad."

The White Witch grinned ferociously. "But it is, and you're afraid. Since the day Marie passed and you realized my role in her death, you have been terrified. Yes, I let the girl die, and it broke my heart. She was sweet and innocent, but no more than any casualty of war. It had to be done."

It was true. For the first time in years, I felt fear. Fear was an unknown: It was as if I looked down a grey corridor of probability and found only blackness, undefined dark matter. I forced a breath. "Please, Emma, tie all this together: Marie. Dresden. My time here with you is limited. Why the senseless killing? The senseless bombing?"

The White Witch released my hand. She stared up at the clouds and fell silent. She did not move. She was motionless for ten seconds, then thirty, a minute, two, three…

Unsettling emotions raged within me. I felt pity for the young girl. I was not without empathy myself. I knew she was suffering. Knowing a White Witch suffers is one thing; witnessing her pain and anguish was a new and unsettling trial. I wanted to get home, and quickly. "Emma. Please."

She nodded and said, "They burned Dresden to punish the Germans; they felt justice by tribunal would be nothing more than a show, a spectacle, a circus for the masses. But mass death, violent death of the innocent, is the purest form of justice or revenge."

She rose to her knees, steadied her trembling body and fixed her lonely stare at me. "Nathan, I hate everything about you and your kind. You're manipulative. You're cruel. Worse, you're vain. Despite all you must endure, you still believe in your work, and the price that others must pay. What price have you paid, Nathan? A life alone? A death devoid of tenderness? A death without a hand to hold?"

"We all have our roles to play, Emma," I said. "I'm truly sorry, but this world was not of my or my associates' making. All I can do, or all we can do, is what we think is best for everyone. Yes, we all must serve our masters, even you. Never doubt our intentions, perhaps imperfect in execution, but not without purpose—survival."

"Now who is delusional?" Emma coughed. Every one of her breaths sounded as if it would collapse her lungs. "Nathan, I know it is you who controls my cancer. Every cell that has metastasized, every tumor, every tortured breath that I have endured is your work." The girl grabbed her book and stood. She wavered a moment and then stepped forward. She was tall for her age, and her eyes met mine. "Nathan, look into your blackened heart and tell me: Are you willing to place all those you love, your sister, your family, all those you hold dear both in this world, this beautiful world of light, and those you must serve in that cynical world of shadow before the fire?"

*

"Nathan, you're staring," the girl said. "You're debating whether I not only have the skill to carry out my threats but also the will to burn this town and that sad dwelling of aged puppet masters into charcoal, not unlike the children of Dresden."

"A White Witch of Empathy does not slaughter," I said firmly. "She protects."

Emma closed her eyes. "Nathan, I am tired. Tomorrow I begin another round of chemo. Nasty, nasty shit. I give you credit. You've picked a virulent and persistent form of cancer."

I did not attempt to hide my pleasure.

Without looking at me, she said, "Nathan, before you go, please understand: You can't wait me out. You can throw all the diseases and medical trials at me that you must. Your anger and your spells are worthless, desperate actions of a cowardly man. I will endure the tumors, the viruses, and the aneurysms— everything. I will survive. I will age. I will get stronger. And then I will carry out what I have threatened. Be certain, I have the will. Now, go. I'm not feeling well. You know—the cancer."

"I will, Emma, but now I want you to remember: Your fight is futile. Your days are limited, even more so than mine."

A short, heavyset woman in white approached us. "Emma, I believe your nurse is summoning you. You must go. But tonight, as you lie alone in your bed, I want you to understand this: You must learn to love your disease. It will be your only love."

As Emma left, holding the arms of her nurse, her steps tentative, I slipped back into a shadow and entered the protective corridors of the Spaces-in-Between, eager to get back among my own, to consult with them how to handle this girl.

I anticipated a long, brutal conflict.

*

Sadly, yes, sadly, I was wrong.

Emma, the terrible White Witch of Empathy, died four months later, succumbing to the disease that she had fought for nearly a year. She died at 3:30 a.m., at Deaconess Memorial, Room 712, accompanied by the rhythmic throbbing of the hospital's ancient radiators and the wind and the hail pounding at the windows.

I had come near midnight, not to gloat, but to witness, and because I had expected she would be alone. The doctors had left her in the care of the nurses, but none of these bitter, indifferent women witnessed the course of Emma's remaining hours. Her adoptive parents, an older couple, were exhausted and had gone home for the evening.

As the night patiently collected Emma's final breaths, Emma did not speak. Nor did I. I watched Emma's skin drain of its blood, leaving a taut, ivory death mask. Her eyes turned a hideous brown, evidence of the poisonous bile spilling throughout her wasted shell. Occasionally, she cast an expressionless glance toward me, but mostly she stared absently forward or toward the windows. Perhaps she still believed she could recover her strength and wage that terrible war she wanted against me.

As I watched the young girl, I could not help but think of what she had said at our first and only discussion: "Why shouldn't I pray for the creature responsible for all this? Hadn't Jesus said to love thine enemy?"

This White Witch deserved to live. Yet, with her ability to enter the forbidden corridors of probability and see a world where White Witches possessed the ability to challenge all that we have held sacred and right, it was best she passed on. The thought of her someday bearing a child sent a deep, cell-crushing chill through me, and this prospect, slim as it might have been, was frightening.

Around 3:00 a.m., Emma moaned and the stench of urine and feces rose from her bed. The final hour had arrived, yet I didn't want Emma to die awash in her own waste. I didn't call for an aide. I knew neither of the old hags would come. The uneducated old women feared Emma; they claimed Emma spoke in tongues, hurling insults at them as they washed the poor girl. Most likely it was just Emma chanting long-forgotten prayers for the departed.

I stood and went to the bathroom. I soaked the bathroom towels in warm water and spent the next fifteen minutes cleaning the waste from Emma, being careful not to offend. Next, I gently turned Emma from side to side and removed the soiled sheets. I replaced the old sheets with new ones from the bed next to us and tucked them snuggly to her chest. Finally, I wiped the sweat from her forehead and cheeks.

After I tossed the dirty linen into the hallway, I closed the door and locked it. I wanted Emma to have the privacy she deserved. When I sat back in my chair, Emma turned her head toward me and said, her voice hoarse and soft, "You missed your calling, Nathan. You would have made a first-rate orderly."

This girl—she would have been interesting to know. "Not really. I don't look good in white."

She smiled, both sad and cynical. "Nathan, will you do me a favor?"

"If I can, I will."

"Always the lawyer," she said. "Please, take my hand."

"Are you sure?"

"Yes. Don't be afraid. I won't hurt you. I can't. I've tried. I've really tried."

I took it. I expected coldness, but it was wonderfully warm, filled with empathy.

"I'm not a bad witch, Nathan," she said. Her breath was acidic, marinated with the bile stench of death. She squeezed my hand. "I'm sorry for some of the things I said—you know, about your personal life."

"It's okay. I understand. I am not without empathy."

Her eyes narrowed. "I would have burned every last soul. Every one of you, even those you love. The good. The innocent. All of them."

"I know."

The warmth in her hand began to dissipate. She started trembling.

"Emma, do you want another blanket?"

She shook her head and drew me close. Her eyes flashed red, and then fell back to grey. In a voice soft and distant, she said, "Is it true, Nathan?"

"Is what true, Emma?"

"Is it true that a White Witch will continue to dream...after she passes?"

"Yes, Emma," I said. "I believe it is so. You will dream."

She released my hand and closed her eyes. "Good," she said, "then, I shall dream. I shall dream of fire."

*

I know the universe as it is constructed is unfair. Why should a young woman such as Emma, a child born to protect other children, suffer and die before reaching adulthood? Doesn't she deserve love and empathy? Family?

If I had an answer I would share, but I have only my purpose and affairs to manage, in the manner that I was taught, and to do so until my end comes forth. It is the best I can do.

If that makes me a coward, then I am exposed.

Emma died fifty odd years ago, and every day I think of her. I also think of a possible future that might have involved a daughter of Emma's, and, like Emma, she may have been a White Witch of Empathy, powerful and deranged, a new breed, blessed with empathy and cursed with vengeance. I think of a future where the age of Wizards is nothing but a long forgotten storm.

And like Emma, I dream.

I dream of fire.

Penetanguishene
Nancy Kay Clark

Maddy and I stand in a clapboard room in a recreated British Naval Base on Penetanguishene Bay. She's pouting, and twisting in her hands that cheap heart pendant the boy I have yet to meet gave her. I've confiscated her cell, so she can't respond to his texts and so she'll pay attention.

We're listening to another teenaged girl whose summer job is to dress up in an 1820 sailor's uniform and interpret the lives of ghosts. This is Miss Letitia's room. There are two slender windows (I wonder if they open) covered by faded lace curtains. The dark-wood canopy bed is too short and squat for twenty-first century tastes. Its straw mattress sags beneath a patchwork counterpane. Beside one of the windows, where the barest bit of light peeks through, sits a small table and two straight-backed chairs. And on the table, as if Miss Letitia had just stepped out for a moment, are a blue-and-white porcelain teacup and saucer and, in a stained oak case, a set of used and dried-out watercolour paints.

A cell rings and a woman rummages through her giant bag. Our guide pauses with a smile fixed to her face. I judge her quickly: a hometown girl, marking time at this summer gig, until she can get the hell out in September, perhaps heading south to go to school in Toronto, or even Montreal. She has a boyfriend, but will move on to more worldly fare when she goes. The woman cannot find her damn cell and, shrugging in apology, leaves.

"You'll notice that Miss Letitia's room connects directly with the bedroom of Captain Roberts and his wife," says our guide, leading the group onwards.

Maddy goes with them, but I lag behind. A faint breeze from the open door has caught the lace at one of the windows, billowing up the fabric and giving it life. I picture the first really warm day of spring; the melt water and April rains had recently receded from the floorboards. Outside the window, the lawn was mud, with bits of new greenery edging forward. A fence, made of spiked lime-washed logs, circled the Captain's house. It was ten feet high. Such a pity, for it obscured the view; a view they had travelled so far to see.

*

"Can we not walk, Rose?" I can hear Letty say. Slim, I imagine, mid-brown hair piled high on her head, a periwinkle blue empire-waisted dress (the kind favoured by Jane Austen heroines), a white pinafore lightly paint-stained. She sat at the table, staring at the fence out the window, neglecting her watercolours.

"Impossible, dear, without an escort," said her sister Rosamund, the Captain's wife. She stood at the other window, teacup and saucer in hand. She was fair-haired, and wore a grass-green dress trimmed with yellow ribbons. She pursed her lips often.

"And the Captain cannot spare anyone today."

"I thought to visit Mrs. Todd." Mrs. Todd was the only other white woman around; she was the wife of Dr. Todd, the assistant surgeon at the base.

"Not today, Letty, but we will see her tonight at our soiree. We will send off Lieutenant Bayfield in style."

"Is he off, then?"

"Tomorrow. I told you that this morning. The ice is finally off the lake, you see."

"He'll be gone for the whole of the summer?"

"Yes. Oh, do not be so gloomy, my dear. The Captain promised a promenade tomorrow up the hill to see the view of the lake...if the weather holds. Won't that be nice?"

*

Midnight, and on the other side of the thin wall, the Captain had finally stopped grunting over Rose. He was now snoring. Letty assumed that Rose was asleep as well, but could not be sure as her sister seemed to barely utter a squeak in bed. Letty, wrapped in the counterpane, waited, waited to be sure. He had kissed her hand. He had—Lieutenant Henry Wolsey Bayfield, Surveyor for the Royal Navy—kissed Letty's hand as he left after the evening's festivities.

She knew she had looked particularly enchanting. She had worn the ruby red evening dress and her grey lace shawl, donned her ivory-coloured gloves, curled her hair in ringlets with a hot iron, rouged her lips, worn her pearls and matching drop earrings. With time to eat up, she had made a five-course meal out of getting ready. She had stretched her toilette so that it would last the whole of the afternoon—planning, choosing, re-choosing (the ruby red or the silver blue?), rehearsing her repartee—dished out in slow morsels to savour.

Letty got out of bed; the quilt still wrapped around her, and pushed her bare feet into her boots. She slipped out of her bedroom, hoping the door wouldn't creak, out of the house and into the yard. She picked her way through the now-cold mud, holding up the hem of her nightgown, and went out the front gate. The Captain's compound stood half way up the hill and the trees had been cleared around it. Letty stayed close to the fence, and looked around. A full moon hung over the lake. She breathed deeply. A breeze caressed her face and whipped back her hair. She shivered.

She was not alone. There was a guard on duty close by. He saw Letty's silhouette in the moonlight, her breath in the air, her hair tumbling about her shoulders, but he did not call out or ask who goes there. She glanced his way. The sailor tilted his head in acknowledgement, but did not approach, said nothing, did nothing.

The guard allowed Miss Letitia these midnight freedoms; she'd been out through the gate before. She never walked very far. It was enough just to be on the other side of the fence for a few minutes at midnight.

Penetanguishene. The name sounded savage on Letty's tongue. The navy purchased the land from the Red Indians, the Captain had said, a perfect spot for a naval base—sheltered and hidden—yet with water deep enough for the largest of lakers.

"Why don't you go with your sister as her companion?" her parents had asked. Letty had not had a successful first season; no offers of marriage had materialized.

"Oh yes, please do come, Letty," Rose had said. "For the Captain will be busy with his duties and you are such good company."

Pen-e-tan-gui-shene. Letty imagined trees and more trees, higher and taller and fatter than any trees in England, a jumble of trees, wherever you looked. She saw rocky cliffs and cold blue water. She saw the most extreme weather; rain and hail, snow and ice, piled on snow and ice and a blasting, riveting wind, which froze your face in an instant. She saw giant bears and slinking wolves and vast birds of prey. She saw Red Indian braves, running through the autumn woods with bare chests and squaws with ebony pigtails down to their bottoms. And she thought, why not?

*

"How bright this world is!" said Letty, her face turned to the wind. Letty and Rose were in the first of five sleighs. They had set out two mornings before, heading north from Fort York. Furniture, linens, flatware, and porcelain, trunks of dresses and bonnets brought all the way from England were piled high on the sleighs. There had been a thaw and then a refreeze—and everything glittered underneath a thin layer of ice.

"Sit down a bit more, dearest, wrap yourself up well. You'll get a chill," Rose said, tucking the furs around her sister's lap. But the wind made Letty smile. The ragged air. The glare of the snow. The blue of the sky. The brown tree trunks and green pine needles.

This world of sharp contrasts pleased Letty more than the creaking, stinking ship of the Atlantic crossing, or the trip on the laker to Fort York.

While Rose sunk further under the furs and seemed to doze, Letty sat straighter in the sleigh. She reveled in the crack of the whip on the horses, the crunch of their hooves in the snow. The caravan of sleighs took the trail into the woods and then out again, the world contracting and expanding. Letty took her gloves off, kept one hand out of her wrappings. She wanted to feel the cold creep into her fingertips. She liked the sweet ache in the bones, and how the skin slowly turned white and then a delicate shade of blue. She liked how, when she could not stand it any longer and finally buried her hand underneath her furs, sharp, prickly heat would envelope the limb.

"How pretty the woods are," said Rose, sleepily; but Letty knew they were so much more. For at any minute, out from the trees could spring a cougar. The great northern woods were home to a whole encyclopedia of dangers, if only they would show themselves.

Late in the afternoon of the fourth day a great expanse of frozen lake came into view. By this time, Letty's bright world had turned dull. The sky hung low with clouds and a relentless sleet poured down. Letty wondered whether she should take off her hat to get the full effect—but Rose probably wouldn't let her.

Captain Roberts came alongside them on horseback.

"Mr. Talbot seems to think we should set up camp on this side of the lake, until the weather clears."

Rose looked around at the pitiful wet woods. "What, here?"

"Perhaps there's a Red Indian encampment nearby," said Letty. "We could take shelter there."

The Captain ignored Letty, and patted his wife's hand. "I think we will brave it, and push on across the lake." It was the worst decision he could have made, but the best one as far as Letty was concerned.

One afternoon, two months later, over tea and whist in the parlour of the Captain's house, Letty recounted the tale to Lieutenant Bayfield in greatest detail.

"We were drenched—simply drenched! The people, the horses, the sleighs, and all our bundles, everything a soggy mess. Oh and that smell of wet wool, the stench of the beaver pelts. Well, I'm sure I don't have to tell you, Sir."

"Letty and I were in the first sleigh, behind us in a line were four others," Rose piped in, not allowing the young officer a comment.

"Piled high with bric-a-brac and crockery," said Letty. "Can you imagine, Lieutenant?" Letty was at her best at these moments. Her eyes were bright; her laughter was contagious. Bayfield was half in love.

Rose felt compelled to point out: "Great Aunt Gertrude's mahogany occasional table with rosewood inlay is hardly bric-a-brac, Letty!"

"And linens and trunk upon trunk upon trunk..."

"It was grandmama's tea service and my embroidered table cloths."

Letty cut in and continued the story: "Well what do you think happened, Lieutenant? We were three-quarters of the way across the lake, when we heard a marvelous crack from behind. I knew what it was immediately. I was expecting it somehow."

Rose cut back in: "The Captain told our driver to keep going, make for the shore as quickly as possible. With all haste, the Captain rode his horse back to help. The horse, as you know Lieutenant, was a beautiful animal: black with white stockings. Trafalgar was its name."

Letty interrupted: "There were screams, yells from the other sleigh drivers, the horses pulling the sleighs were screaming. We were craning our necks back to see behind us, the sleet and slush in our eyes. Two sleighs, it looked like, had fallen through the ice. The men were trying frantically to cut the horses free so they would not fall through. There was one sleigh on its side; all Rose's bundles strewn everywhere."

"And then my dear, beloved Captain..." said Rose in a high squeak.

"Suddenly disappeared!" declared Letty.

"I could not breathe. I could not see my dearest," Rose said in such a dramatic whisper that Bayfield had to lean forward to hear her.

"We learnt later that Trafalgar had tripped and slid on the ice. Horse and rider went down. There was another enormous crack. Another sleigh sank. The Captain got up. He tried to get Trafalgar up. But the horse was injured; it would not move. The ice all around was cracking. The Captain took out his pistol..." At this point, with Bayfield at the edge of the settee, Letty stood up to mime the action: cocking the imaginary pistol, pointing it at the imaginary prone horse.

Rose sobbed into her hanky. "The sound of that shot."

"He had no choice, Rose. It was either that or let the poor horse drown. By this time, our sleigh had made it to shore, along with the second. The men, with what horses they could save, scrambled across the lake."

"All my linen and porcelain..."

"Three sleighs full, but thankfully none of the men."

Bayfield murmured his agreement.

"Trafalgar and four other horses, all gone, down into a watery grave."

"Letty," said Rose, sipping her lukewarm tea. "You make that sound almost desirable."

*

After Bayfield left with his survey crew that summer, life for the Roberts women shrank. The Captain was busy and could not keep them company as much as he professed to have liked. May dragged into June and July. Sometimes it was too hot and sometimes too cold. Sometimes it was too dry and sometimes too wet. And most of the time too full of biting insects to keep the windows open. At first, Letty thought she might help Mrs. Todd and her husband, the surgeon. One afternoon, she raced into the dining room, where Rose sat eating luncheon alone.

"Letty, where have you been?"

"I went to visit Mrs. Todd."

"Letty!"

"Oh, do not scold, Rose. I took a guard. Only Mrs. Todd was not there. She had already left to assist Dr. Todd at the hospital. There has been an accident at the shipyards. I have this on reliable authority; I met Mr. Talbot on the way. Apparently, an astronomically large pile of logs had gotten loose. The logs rolled down the hill and landed on top of several men, crushing limbs and vital organs."

"Oh how horrid! Where are you going, Letty?"

"I must change into appropriate attire."

"Appropriate attire for what?"

"Why to help attend the wounded at the hospital, of course."

"Oh, Letty, I'm not certain that you should."

"But I must, there is talk of amputations!"

"But Mrs. Todd is there."

"Mr. Talbot assured me there are more than enough wounded for the both of us."

"Letty, I am sure Mr. Talbot said no such thing. What you fail to understand is that Mrs. Todd is accustomed to such work. Being born and raised in Lower Canada, she is tough in character. You, however, are not. It is too much for your constitution."

"Rose! It is my Christian duty. Besides I know I will be very good with severed limbs."

"Letty, the Captain will not approve."

Rose was right, Captain Roberts did not approve.

*

As July slid into August, Letty spent most of her days sitting in the parlour, working on her embroidery. Rose was not much company. Things had become heated in the Captain's bedroom. Letty could not quite hear the muffled conversations through the wall, but she could hear the tone of voice. It would start out plaintive and imploring; this was Rose. There would be a taciturn reply from the Captain. Rose would start again, but now her voice was higher pitched, a little more insistent. Again, the Captain would reply, but it would not satisfy Rose. And she would make a third attempt and then a fourth, until the Captain invariably shouted: "Confounded woman, be still!" And Rose was heard sobbing.

Letty tried to talk to Rose about it, to be useful, to give comfort; but when it came to her husband, Rose would not confide. Mornings of bare conversations between the sisters melded into silent afternoons, until one day in August, Letty absent-mindedly pricked her finger with her embroidery needle. She liked it: the surprise, the sharp pain, the swift hiss under her breath. She pricked her finger again; her heart fluttered. She looked over at her sister, who was staring out the window at the fence. Letty took her needle and jammed it into her finger until it throbbed and the blood pooled out and dripped onto to the white embroidery. She sucked at the blood like a vampire.

That night there was a tremendous thunderstorm. Lightning lit up the rooms; thunder rattled the clapboards and rain pounded on the roof. All was silent from the room next door, as if one storm had melted the other. But Letty could not sleep. She hated her room. She could not stand the bed, the patchwork counterpane, the lace curtains, the prim table with its two chairs, her watercolours. She wanted to be outside. Outside the fence. She wanted to feel the rain on her face and between her breasts. She wanted to feel the mud on the souls of her feet. It had been so long since her last midnight freedom.

She got out of bed. She left the counterpane and her boots behind, and did not care whether the door creaked. In her thin nightgown, in her bare feet, with the rain already seeping through the floorboards, she left her room, she left the house, she left the yard, she went through the gate, to the other side of the fence. She did not stop at the fence. Shrieking, she raced down the hill toward the lake.

The guard on duty saw Letty run, in a flash of lightning, like a mad ghost, her hair in a soggy mess and her white nightie wet and plastered to her body in such an embarrassing way that the guard could not help but stare.

He caught up to her before she could pitch herself into the water. He dragged her struggling body back to the Captain's house.

Rose dried her off and put her back to bed. Someone fetched Dr. Todd and soon a diagnosis was declared: Hysteria Nervosa, a woman's complaint. She was given laudanum and slept for days.

*

When our tour of the base is over, we thank our guide and Maddy and I leave. In the car, Maddy puts in her earbuds and is lost in Justin Beiber. As I pay the parking attendant, I plot Letty's escape.

Perhaps, when the last of the sightseers leaves her room today, Ghost Letty will find that woman's cell phone. Perhaps Letty will figure out how to surf the net on it and Google a map of Ontario's highway system. Perhaps she steals some money from the teenaged tour guide. Perhaps she'll put on her boots, sneak out of the base in her nightie, and hitchhike to town. It could happen. It's more doable now, since there are fewer woods and more roads than when she was alive.

I stop at Tim Hortons outside Midland so Maddy can use the toilet, and I can get a coffee. As I wait in line, a noise catches my attention. I turn to look. It's just my imagination, I'm sure. But I see a vapour-thin Letty running through the door, right through a dozen oblivious people and up to the counter.

"Help me! Hide me!" she yells at the uniformed girl at the cash. "They're right behind me. I can't go back, please." She grabs the girl's hand with her insubstantial one. The girl doesn't notice.

"What can I get for yous?" the girl asks the man in front of me.

Ghost Letty and I turn to look back at the entrance. We see a terrifying sight. The ghosts of Dr. Todd and Captain Roberts barge in and head straight for Letty.

"Help me! Help me!" Letty cries, but no one hears her. She wraps her arms around the Plexiglas doughnut display and holds on.

"Now Letitia, be reasonable," says the Captain. "We're not going to hurt you. Please, be a good girl and come with us. You are not well."

But Ghost Letty will not budge. She plants her feet as firmly as a ghost can. She shakes her head back and forth, back and forth, back and forth. "No. No. No."

Dr. Todd grabs her shoulders in his beefy hands and pulls. The Captain grabs her waist. I am the only witness to this assault, but am helpless to intervene.

I step up to the counter to place my order.

Jenny Can't
Go Back to Bismarck
Frank T. Sikora

You would think if you left your twin toddlers drowning in the basement wash sink you wouldn't go to the casino to throw your grocery money on the slots. Yet, not more than two hours after the little buggers took their last water-filled breaths, Jenny Simpson of Bismarck, North Dakota, slipped on her best jeans and favorite satin blouse and the pearl earrings her grandmother had left her and drove thirty hilly miles to the Prairie Nights Casino. Jenny looked good, too—perhaps she was a bit too thin and perhaps she wore too much blue eye shadow and, if you looked closely at her arms, you'd see needle marks—but she definitely turned heads.

You would also think after committing a double infanticide you'd have a degree of paranoia wailing like a siren deep in your moral center; yet, Jenny weaved her way through the herd of obese, cheaply dressed, chain smoking, and oh-so-hopeful degenerates towards her favorite slot machine, the Mad Hatter, feeling optimistic about her future and mercifully free from her current boyfriend's anger management issues associated with his inability to hold a job or an erection.

Jenny settled onto the stool before the Mad Hatter's maniacal neon eyes and pulled a bagful of quarters out of her purse. She shot the woman to her right a cursory smile and immediately began dropping quarter after quarter into the Hatter's belly, prepared to collect the $199,999.99 jackpot the machine's fancy ass graphics promised.

The slot machine's lights flashed; its bells clanged. The Mad Hatter's animated arms flailed in computer-generated precision. But the Hatter not only failed to drop the 200 grand into her lap, it refused to disburse so much as a quarter back into Jenny's slender hands. Undaunted, Jenny reached into her purse and removed the stack of reserve quarters as well as her grandfather's silver dollars, which had been hidden in a secret pocket beneath her wallet and birth control pills.

The results were the same. Driven by cruel algorithms, the tumblers turned and fell and quickly drained Jenny of more than $100, quite a sum for a waitress who worked the late shift at the International House of Pancakes.

Now, at this point, you would think Jenny would consider her situation: the outrage sure to come from her family and community, her dwindling funds and, of course, the moral implications of her actions, but Jenny simply bit down hard on her lip and considered her plan, which she believed was going so well. She ran her hand along the Mad Hatter's face and said, "I've kept my part of the bargain. Keep yours."

A series of red lights within the Mad Hatter's eyes flickered, but it remained silent. Such arrogance, Jenny thought as she turned to the large, red-haired woman crushing the stool next to her. Jenny noticed the woman's change bucket overflowed with quarters and silver dollars. Jenny leaned over toward the woman and said, "You're having a nice night."

The woman ignored Jenny and poured quarter upon quarter into the grey belly of her machine, The Cat in the Hat.

"Excuse me, I'm speaking to you," Jenny said.

The big woman glanced at Jenny, spat out her gum, turned back to her machine and pressed the "pull" switch. Silver dollars flooded out of the cat's hat into the woman's bucket and onto the floor.

Jenny felt her anger rising. She rummaged through her purse for a vial of coke; a quick line would be nice right now; perhaps a little infusion of crank—crystal methamphetamine—anything to keep a tighter edge. Just in case, Jenny told herself, I feel the urge to put the bitch down.

Sadly, Jenny found nothing, just her last five quarters. "What makes you special?" Jenny yelled at the woman. "You think you're better than me? Look at you. You're gross. You're a worm. If you weren't wearing shoes, I wouldn't be able to tell your head from your ass."

The woman swayed as if caught in a tremor, then stood, grabbed her bucket of coins and lumbered away, her massive butt swaying from side to side.

Clearly, now you would expect Jenny to reconsider her situation. Sure, her little tantrum made her feel better, but her plan had taken a detour. She had lost focus. She had lost most of her money, and given that she left a note stating, "Good Riddance," on the post of the boys' twin beds, the police might be looking for her. Maybe I should keep moving, she thought. Instead, Jenny leaned close to the Mad Hatter, her warm breath gracing the machine. "You owe me," Jenny whispered. "I deserve a reward, for all my sacrifices—my health, my dignity, and most of all my youth, and isn't that more precious than anything?"

Jenny shuddered thinking about the endless hours and days wasted with her miserable little boys. At least that part of the plan had worked perfectly. They'd hardly fought. Just thrashed a little at the end. Their eyes had darted back and forth, but they hadn't suffered. Not really.

With grim, pinched face determination, Jenny reached down into her purse and snatched her remaining quarters. She dropped all five of them into the slots, grabbed the lever, and paused. What if this doesn't work? she thought. What if the Mad Hatter fails me? Then what?

Jenny rubbed her sweaty hands along her hips. She glanced down at her legs. Yes, she thought with a smile, I'll always have my body. I've used it before. I've kept myself fit. I'm not part of the herd eating my way to an early grave, killing myself with selfish indulgence. With this body, I can go anywhere. I can find another man if I want. I could make a living dancing. That's not so bad, is it? Another smile. Yes, I can go anywhere. I just can't go back to Bismarck.

Jenny pulled the lever. The Mad Hatter laughed and spilled out a rushing pile of quarters and silver dollars.

Jenny screamed: so loud and so hard and so full of joy. Happily alone, a wonderfully wide world awaited her.

Unravel the ties...

"I'll lend you my Bible and you can read all the bits they don't want you to read"

The Song of Solomon

Birds of a Feather

Phyllis Humby

I promised the doctor I'd stay off booze. It messes me up. Especially with the meds. Besides, I need a clear head.

The corner of my mouth lifts in a thank you as the waiter approaches the table with my order. At the first sip of the pale wine, my nose wrinkles in distaste. Maybe disgust. Even a full-bodied Shiraz is preferable over a sweet blush. A stiff drink—whiskey or vodka—would be better. But the good stuff is out of bounds. The rim of the glass met my lips again. This *fruit juice* can't really be considered drinking. I slip a couple of pills into my mouth and take another sip.

Ignoring the surrounding tables, particularly the one where the old guy sits, I grab my purse and head for the door labeled *Women*.

Dim lighting casts unflattering shadows on the reflection in the mirror. I lean close and massage the puffiness under my eyes. Smooth the lines on my cheeks. For a 50-year-old, this face looks pretty good. Too bad I'm thirty-five. It's stress, I tell myself, ignoring the years of self-abuse and confinement. If nothing turns up in the town records today, the search is over.

I paint some colour onto my nearly invisible lips and sweep blush along my cheekbones.

My need to know consumes me. As a kid, I believed everything she told me. Daddy's dead. We moved away for a fresh start. No relatives. No photos. No visits back home. How likely is that scenario? The trouble is, by the time I was old enough for more questions, Mom was at the bottom of the lake.

I wriggle my makeup back into my bag and tug at the zipper until the tissue jamming it is worked free. It doesn't matter how big my purse is, it's always crammed full.

Nothing makes sense. Too many damn secrets. A crazy lady looks back at me from the mirror. *No, not crazy. Not crazy.*

One small clue indicates that Mom lived in this rinky-dink town at one time. Maybe I did too. So far, there's no trace of us here. She must have changed our names. But why? Why would she do that? Witness protection is the only thing I can think of, and that comes from watching too much TV.

My fingers knead a circle against my temples. I can't risk being locked up again.

I jerk open the restroom door and return to the dining room. The table beside mine is empty. The old guy who'd followed me through town for most of the morning has finally given up. He's gone. Who was he and why was he following me? *I'm not paranoid. I'm not.*

He was in the park. The playground, actually. I was taking a shortcut and noticed him on a bench near the swings—hunched over, elbows on his knees, head craned forward. Later, while walking past a store, I glanced at the window and could see his reflection behind mine. It didn't make me nervous, just wary.

For the most part, I'd ignored him. That is, until he followed me into the restaurant. That creeped me out. There was a *Wait to be Seated* sign just inside the door. I veered around it and chose a table in the centre of the dining room. He, too, disregarded the sign. The stranger sat across from me, along the wall. Close enough to witness the involuntary dance of my fingers against the tabletop. *I'm not imagining this.*

Anxiety has been my enemy forever. Mostly, the meds help. This man, this town, and the fact that nobody here wants to answer my questions makes me jumpy, that's all.

So I ordered that watery wine and took slow even breaths.

I'm pecking at my salad, thankful that the stalker hasn't returned, when the waiter brings me another glass of wine.

"The man who was sitting over there," I nod in the direction of the empty table. "Did he say anything to you before he left?"

Dropping the professional patter, he tells me, "He didn't order. Said he was waiting for someone. Must have figured they weren't coming. He left."

The waiter looks to be in his early twenties. If he were old, like maybe sixty, I'd show him the picture of my mother and ask if he remembers her. Instead, I say, "Do you know the man? Have you seen him before?"

"Yeah." He shifts from one foot to the other. His tone changes from proficient server to that of someone sharing an intimacy. "When I was a kid, I used to see him all the time at the park. He was always hanging around." He chuckles at my alarmed expression. "He wasn't dangerous or anything. He's just not all there. Cross. I think that's his name. Or maybe that's just what the kids call him."

Not all there. I wonder if that's what attracted the weirdo to me. Birds of a feather and all that. I bunch the paper napkin in my hand.

When I'd glanced over at his table earlier, he was shifting sideways in his chair. We locked eyes. His expression was scary. Like he was looking right through me. I might have jumped up and left the restaurant if the waiter hadn't approached. Good timing.

I spear another spinach leaf and piece of bacon. My appetite kicks in, and though the stranger lingers in my mind, I enjoy every delicious morsel. Another stolen glance and I see his table is still unoccupied. A relieved sigh passes my lips and my shoulders shrug away the tension.

How had the waiter described him? The local crazy. Every town has one. A thought screeches through my mind. Will that be me one day? Is that what my hometown will say? *Helpmehelp-mehelpme* I feel my lips move and cover my mouth hoping no one heard.

"Another glass of wine?" The young server is standing next to the table watching my fingers circle the rim of the empty glass.

Tucking a limp strand of hair behind my ear, I study him. Sometimes I think my past is written all over me for everyone to see. Do I look to him like someone who's spent three years in the loony bin?

"No. Just my bill." My voice sounds harsh. I blame the wine.

I'm convinced that he's giving me the same stare as the others—the ones who whisper behind my back. Just like they did in high school. That's when it all started. My so called 'mental health issues'. At first it was the nightmares. I would see my mother's car going into the lake. Hear her screams for help. I'd see and hear everything. That's the 'crazy' part. I wasn't even there when it happened. I was home with the Cotters the night of my mother's accident. A little ten-year-old kid. Orphaned.

By the end of my teens, alcohol was my drug of choice. It was either anesthetize myself or give in to ultimate despair. That had only one ending.

I was convinced that the nightmares would end and that gnawing ache would go away if only I could find out why my mother and I were on the run. The anxiety attacks would stop. The drinking would stop. If only I could learn the truth. But how?

When the Cotters sold the store to move south, they forwarded an old trunk of my mother's personal things. A search for legal documents turned up nothing. It wasn't until I was packing for my move into a new place that I carefully examined the contents. An apron with embroidered strawberries. Print blouses and skirts. Even shoes with the heels worn down and toes scuffed. A multitude of drawings and cards from when I was old enough to hold a crayon. There were also cookbooks. Inside one of them was an envelope. An empty envelope. Addressed to Mom. On one side was a recipe scribbled in pencil. But it was the postmark on the other side that most interested me. *Trowbridge*. Someone who lived in Trowbridge had written to my mom. I tossed everything out of the trunk looking for the letter. No luck.

The Town of Trowbridge was a three-hour drive or four-and-a-half hour bus ride from Westmont County, where we'd settled with the Cotters. Trowbridge could be my birthplace. Or maybe not. But someone from that town knew her. My hands covered my face as I gave in to emotions I'd held in check for too long. Could this really bring me peace of mind? It felt like a gift from my mother.

It was a two-hour flight from where I now lived to the airport closest to Trowbridge. Humming with excitement, I'd steered my rental vehicle towards the town. The thrill got old fast. No record of my mother having lived in Trowbridge. And, so far, no birth record for me, either.

The server slides my bill onto the table and indulges in idle chatter as he clears the dishes. When he walks away, my breath catches. The local eccentric is back. His aftershave lingers as he passes. I fumble with my wallet, leave money on the table, and make a beeline for the exit.

As I hustle in the direction of the Sandman Motel where I'd left my car, the smell of diesel fuel from the truck idling at the traffic light fills my lungs. My head throbs with the sound of a baby's squalls. Children shout as they brush past me, their legs pumping and their feet pounding against the pavement towards the playground in the park. The playground where that psycho sat earlier this morning. The main street feels safer than taking that shortcut again and I hurry along the sidewalk towards the motel.

My pace quickens at the sight of my car. The minute I slide inside, I engage the locks and the ignition. My knuckles whiten against the steering wheel.

It's the wine. Alcohol triggers my paranoia. Just like Dr. Garrett said. I tug the phone from my purse. My finger hovers over his number. I can already hear that snooty whine. 'Tina, how many times have we been through this? You know the risks when you combine your medication with alcohol and I don't have to remind you that ...' Blah, blah, blah! I toss the phone onto the passenger seat.

Eyeballing the parking lot for danger, I drop the gear into reverse, wheel out of the reserved space in front of my room, and accelerate towards the street. Pressing through amber traffic lights, my instincts scream to pack up and go home. Ignoring my twisted gut, I swerve to the side of the road, stop, and program Westmont County into the GPS. I pull a U-ey and head in the direction of my earliest childhood memory—Cotter's Grocery Store. When I was a toddler, my mother had found a job there and we'd lived in the apartment upstairs. It was the place I called home for my formative years. I can't leave without seeing it. My breathing slows and my heart rate is nearing normal.

When I get close, even though I'm braced for change, it hurts to see the modernized storefront. The upper storey windows show signs of inhabitants. Greenery grows from pots on the sills. A window propped open. Bright tangerine coloured curtains. When my tires kiss the curb, I shut off the engine and lean my head back against the seat. Remembering so much. Yet not enough.

Minutes pass before I get out of the car. Stepping inside the store, I foolishly listen for the tinkle of the door chime. Biting my bottom lip, I walk the muted aisles, missing the creak of old hardwood. My throat tightens and I worry that coming here is a mistake. The heavy dullness feels like bricks piled one by one on top of my head. I can't let the panic overtake me here. Not in front of these people, strangers. I edge over to the corner of the store at the end of the aisle and close my eyes. *Inhale. Exhale. Calm.*

The air conditioning, gleaming chrome, and tile floors disappear. The only grandma I ever had, Nana Cotter, bustles up the aisle in her cotton shift, blue-gray hair combed into a tidy French roll. My mother's voice calls from the front of the store and both women laugh. Dust mites tickle my nose in the musty warm surroundings as I clean the tops of canned goods stacked along the shelves. I see things in the store that I hadn't thought of in years. The bins of candies and chocolate bars near the front door. The squeak of the revolving rack that held paperback novels. Papa's apron, stained from his duties behind the meat counter...

A clash of grocery carts startles me back to the present. My head turns from side to side expecting staring eyes and whispered comments. Though no one is watching me, I feel spooked and bolt for the door. Everything is soaring out of control. I'm scared. *I'm not crazy!* It's hours before I get back to Trowbridge, emotionally and physically drained. The parking lot of the Sandman is quiet with only a handful of empty cars in sight.

Inside my room with the bolt lock in place, I feel relief. Then realize I've forgotten my phone in the car. *Shit!* I unlock my door, dash outside, grab it off the passenger seat, and race back.

By the time I search the room—the bathroom and closet are empty, no one's under the bed—I'm a quivering mess with a runny nose and tears dripping from my chin. I dump the contents of my purse onto the bed and find what I need. With the slightest hesitation, I toss a pill to the back of my throat and dry swallow.

When I shove aside the stuff from my purse and sit on the bed, a mini bottle of vodka rolls against my hip. The silver and red label as alluring as a lover. *No alcohol.* My fingers stroke the bottle. *Alcohol and meds.* Twisting the cap, I drain the two ounces in one gulp and lie back on the bed. My eyes close. I feel I could sleep for a month. But then it seems as if only minutes have gone by when I awake. My body feels like a pincushion. Sharp needles poking me everywhere.

I push off the bed and begin to pace. Back and forth. Moving quicker with each turn. Short rapid steps. Rubbing my arms. Tugging at my hair. It's not my fault—the wine was practically Kool-Aid, and only a couple of glasses. The vodka bottle winks at me from the side of the bed. I grab it and toss it against the wall.

My mind shatters. Every fruitless moment spent in Trowbridge comes back as if my brain is on fast rewind. What didn't make any sense before is brilliantly clear now. More than once I'd been mistaken for someone named Alice.

Alice, I repeat to myself. Alice must be my mother's real name. Maybe I look like her. I finger comb my hair into place and turn to the mirror. A mascara-streaked drunkard's mask taunts me. *No, no.*

ImustleaveImustleaveImustleave. Nearly undone with panic, my back and forth pacing continues until it shortens to three or four steps in each direction. *I'm hallucinating.* My hands squeeze into fists. My brain is on overload. As often happens, fatigue takes over and my eyes are rolling in my head as I try to fight it off. Exhausted, I lie back on the bed.

On the brink of twilight, I hear my mom's voice. And my own little-kid voice. They echo off the high ceilings of our apartment. In my sleep state, I try to hold it together but I know I'm losing it. I'm losing my mind. My arms and legs weigh too much to move. Tears slide from my eyes and trail towards the pillow. This is another breakdown. I know it is. And I can't. I can't go back to that place. The blankets muffle my gulping sobs until I fall asleep.

The room phone wakes me. Sweat is pooled between my breasts and my tongue is glued to the roof of my mouth. It takes some fumbling to untangle myself from the blankets and stumble to the desk. *Hello?* It sounds like a frog's croak.

A smoke-ravaged voice rumbles, "Alice?"

My head clears at the sound of this demented person.

"I am *not Alice!* I'm Tina Strong. Please. Leave me alone."

Imagining the creepy-looking stalker hunched over his phone, I shudder and hang up. This can't be happening. Cold sweat beads my face and I pull a blanket from the bed, wrap up in it, and drop into the chair.

I look at my phone then realize I have no one to call. The motel phone rings again. "Creep!" I say, my anger overtaking the fear. "Who is this? You son of a bitch! Who are you?"

Nothing but the sound of sobbing and moaning.

"Listen to me, you blubbering maniac, I'm not who you think I am. You're scaring the hell out of me. Stop it!" My voice is screech level. The dial tone buzzes in my ear.

Remembering his tortured eyes staring at me in the restaurant gives me the shakes. In the tomb-like quiet of the room, my heart pounds. It's happening. The Dread. The Panic. I'll hyperventilate. Drop to my knees. Gasp for breath. That's the way it always goes.

Calm. Down. Relax. Breathe.

Time passes. It could be fifteen minutes or three hours. My movements are jerky and unnatural when I stand.

Under the stark light of the bathroom, I wish I looked only as bad as I thought I had in the restaurant mirror earlier in the day. Was that today? I'm no longer sure of the passage of time. Mascara and tears swirl down the drain with the soapy residue rinsed from my face. The porcelain is cool to the touch and I want to curl inside the sink and let the water overflow. The irony of having a shower stall in these rooms rather than a bathtub is not lost on me.

I swing my suitcase onto the bed and begin to pack. Within seconds, the dresser and closet are empty. Not bothering to fill the toiletry bags, I gather and dump handfuls of loose makeup and hair products on top of my clothes, zip up the bag, and leave it by the door.

Pushing my hair back off my face, I scan the room for anything I've forgotten. Desperate to go home—too terrified to leave—I sit on the edge of the chair, arms hugging my body. When I realize that I'm rocking back and forth, it reminds me of being in the institution. Being trapped there seems preferable to waiting here.

I get up and double-check the lock. Secure. Then I curl up on the bed, try to calm myself, and think through everything that's happened. Despite my frame of mind, it starts to make sense.

I'm certain now that Alice is my mother. That man on the phone must have known her. The waiter…didn't he say that guy was always the town crazy? Yeah, he did say that. Well, that crazy person probably stalked my mother. No wonder she ran away.

I lurch to my feet and begin another round of aimless motion. I want the questions to stop. But they keep coming. One after the other. *Was Alice a single mom who needed a fresh start? Had Dad really died in a construction accident when I was born? Maybe that's when this man started stalking Mom. Maybe he was responsible for my dad's accident. Yes. That's it. He went crazy with guilt. Wouldn't leave my mother alone. She had to take me. Run away. Adopt new names so he couldn't find us. Stop! Stop!* My stomach is queasy and I swallow to keep from racing to the bathroom.

The police are my only way out of this town and away from that person. They can give me an escort. I smack my forehead. Why hadn't I thought of that earlier? Before I even reach the phone, something occurs to me. They might do a background check and find out I've spent time in an asylum. A paranoid schizo. They'll think I'm imagining all of this. I begin to laugh. And laugh. I laugh until my eyes are wet. Yes, of course, that's it. My paranoia. *I am imagining this.* None of this is real. I take gulping breaths as the relief washes over me.

My stomach drops at the sound of the telephone. Second ring. Third ring. I pinch my arm. *I'm only imagining this!* Four rings.

"Hello?"

"You always come back. I see you everywhere."

Unable to control my hysteria, I cry out, "Why is this happening to me?" I'm still raving when I hang up on him.

I think of Dr. Garrett and replay his calming tone. *Inhale. Exhale.*

It's a bad dream. Hallucinations. It's happened before. I just need to make it to morning. *Dammit Tina, get hold of yourself!*

Weak with fatigue, I pull off my clothes and crawl under the covers. My eyes close as an old song tries to play in my mind. I fall asleep before I remember the lyrics.

*

A brilliant beam burns through my closed eyes. I squint against the intensity of the ceiling light. My brain is in a fog and I don't know where I am. Disoriented, I prop myself up to peer around the room. The motel. I remember.

And then. My mind screams. *Wake up! Wake up! Wake up!*

The curtain billows from the gaping window. He came through the...

In a flash it's clear. I. am. not. dreaming.

My mouth opens in a guttural shriek. I pull my legs under me and scramble onto my knees. In a crouched position, I catapult from the bed.

He stands between the door and me. Nowhere to run. No way to escape.

I jockey from side to side.

"How did you survive? I forced your car into the lake. No way, Alice. There's no way you survived that." His slurred words rupture into staccato puffs of air.

The lake? My mother's car accident?

"Oh God. Please don't. Don't hurt me." I plead for my life. *Don't do this. Don't hurt me.* Even to my ears, the words sound like the *waaa waaa* of a bawling infant.

He moves forward, his arms open in an embrace. Only it isn't a loving gesture. It's certain death. The knife glints in the overhead light as it rises above me.

We both sink to the floor.

His eyes are pools of distress and a sour reek descends on me as he pulls me close.

My insides are burning yet my body shakes with icy cold. I've never fought harder in my life without moving an inch. I don't want to die.

The moment is surreal. I smell the fresh night air through the open window. Hear the plop of his tears against my cheeks. Feel them slide down my face. In slow motion, my eyelids open and close. The sound is like the shutter of an old camera. A snapshot.

Images roll through my mind like black and white pictures on a movie reel. I'm bouncing in my mother's arms as she runs up the gravel road. My fingers tug at the tangles in her hair.

Frame by frame, memories return. A man tosses me in the air. Catches me. I giggle. "More, more," I tell him. He tosses me again. And again.

It's getting harder to breathe. The pain is a scalding iron pressed against my skin.

His fingers dig into my shoulders as he lifts me from the floor and rocks me in his arms. "Alice, you should never have taken my baby girl. Where is Christine, Alice?"

I know who he is. I know who I am. My lips move to form the word. He leans closer...

One Mad Sweetheart

Steve Nelson

Everything was fine until she turned crazy on me. I couldn't ditch her—first, because she wouldn't let me; second, because she'd been on an even keel when we'd started off so I figured I was partly responsible for her demise. I knew we wouldn't last but thought maybe I could rehabilitate her well enough to sic her on some other foolish Romeo. But it wasn't long before she could sense the new temporary way I looked at her. First she tried to be sweet and chummy, but I wasn't buying. Then she offered to expand our repertoire. I'd never even thought to ask for some of the things she said she'd do. I knew she hadn't done them either because we'd been together since we were young. "It won't change things," I told her. Still, she said we should try. So we tried, but didn't get far. Talking about it beforehand had ruined it for me. I knew I was being devilish myself, but I still had some principles rattling about inside me.

Sometimes I'd stay out late—just to breathe. One night I rolled in and she was naked on the couch, knees to chin, every inch of her scissor-sliced, little pink welts rising up like she'd been wrapped in wire mesh for days. This was before cutting was in vogue. She was a real trendsetter. And only the week before, she'd reupholstered that very couch, saying to me, See? See what a nice, little sanewoman I can be?

"You don't love me anymore," she sobbed.

Of course I'd told her so already, but instead of reminding her, I just said, "You should talk to someone." Meanwhile I was asking myself, how did a nice kid like me end up here? I'd already stopped asking myself what had happened to the nice girl she'd been—not wanting to know the answer. But she wouldn't talk with anyone, fearing they'd diagnose her crack-brained like her dad before her. I figured she'd end up a kitchen drunk like her mum if something didn't happen. But nothing did. She couldn't hold a job. I was delivering Chinese food. We were broke. We'd fight. We'd screw, but every time afterwards I'd tell myself never again—the fear of being shackled to her and future mad little kids too much to bear. Still, I was weak. If she had any warmth left in her, it was deep inside, and I needed something to help me forget about all my gloom and heartache and spite.

My mom would call regularly and ask, "How are you doing?"

"Everything's good," I'd tell her. "Everything's great."

*

Life dragged on. My little sweetheart dyed her hair black, then cut it short, then dyed it red then black again. There were more fights. More pleading. More deals with her and myself. I'd get an occasional gulp of air, but it was getting to be so it wasn't enough.

One night she took my books and cut them to pieces. She'd already snipped the life from my cassette tapes, but that I could handle, because I knew I'd be switching over to CDs soon enough. But there was no going back from this. She'd gotten Hemingway, Vonnegut, even good old Somerset Maugham. That night as she slept, I snuck out, leaving a note saying it was done, done, done. Cowardly I know, but sometimes life leaves you no choice.

I drove halfway across the state to my friend's house. "What a surprise," he said.

"Just needed to get away," I told him, but by the next day she'd tracked me down and was bringing her scowling mug to see me on the afternoon bus. I wanted to drive halfway across the country, but then my friend would be stuck with her. I got drunk instead. She arrived. We argued. We drove back home, spitting at each other all the way. She broke my windshield. I broke her glasses. Everything we could break, we broke. But still it wasn't enough.

Finally though, back at our place, she said, "You don't love me anymore." But it wasn't an accusation this time. She knew it finally and looked at me with blank eyes, then got up and walked across the parking lot alone. For a second I felt almost sad that it was really over, but then I said to myself: Leave, go while you can, you fool! And as I drove away and felt myself begin to breathe again, I told myself: Whatever you do, don't ever do that again, none of it. And I never have, and I never will, because one mad sweetheart is all one needs in life. One mad sweetheart is more than enough.

Night at the Store
Steve Nelson

While I am reminiscing, I've got one more funny story about this strange time in my life. One night that summer my little nutcase put on a dress of all things and came down to the grocery store with me. The dress was a musty, brown, plaid, to-the-knees number she'd gotten from a secondhand store some months earlier. I could see, as we were cutting across the street outside our building, that she considered herself a real fashion plate or something—a grungy beauty queen.

Now, the mere presence of her blonde mop outside the quiet horrors of our dusty little pad was already an event, as it had been some time since she'd seen a face besides my angry mug and maybe Oprah's. What inspired her return to the world I didn't know, and didn't care. I just wanted to get our stuff and get back home. All we needed was some essentials: milk and bread and cereal and applesauce and fruit cocktail, which was the sort of things we pretty much lived on that summer, what with our lack of money, and all the running I was doing, and our general heartache and misery. I wish I was going over the top with this, but I'm not. This is the real dope so far, the real squeal.

Anyway, we got to the store, a little family joint three blocks over from our place, and within a minute or two had all our loot, and I just wanted to check out and get home, have a late night bowl of Cheerios. But no, get this, my little mademoiselle decides to stop at the magazine rack, picks one up, begins flipping through it; then she just stands there, calm as can be, perusing the pages like everything was casual and fine and we were just a sweet loving couple out at one of our regular haunts, just killing time happily.

I began to wish I'd gone out alone, and, in fact, to my other grocery store, the Shop-Rite a few blocks further the other way. It was a bigger and cheaper operation, but really I went there (I guess I can tell you) because there was this sultry check-out girl working there, and she was always giving me the eye. I mean throwing the real smoldering goo at me, and I was pitching it back to her too and gladly, gladly. This girl always wore a lot of dark eye makeup, lipstick on her big lips, and was pieced together like the puzzle of my dreams—but seriously, was lean and mean in a Mediterranean sexpot kind of way. Everything but the girl next door, and I imagined her all sorts of ways, bent this way, then that, her mouth all over me, and my hands digging into her angles.

All my life I'd been a fool for check-out girls and waitresses and stuff like that, but this was something more. Even though we never talked beyond restrained hellos and the necessary exchanges of money, that whole summer, walking out afterwards across the dirty parking lot outside the store, I would sigh dreamily like we'd been in a big clench together.

Some days, when things were really coming down on me, really closing in, I'd even make extra trips to the store for one or two items—like aspirin or toothpaste or razor blades—just to see her, get one of those combustible looks from her to give me a start, keep me going or from going over.

But, of course, she wasn't always there, and after a while she kind of cooled towards me, got a little tired, I suppose, of me and my dumb face staring drop-jawed at her, licking my lips, and swallowing nervously. She probably wanted me to say something to her—just something like: "Hey. Hi. How are you today?" Acknowledge her in some way at least. She was just a check-out girl at an East Side grocery store, not really a dreamy Sophia Loren returned to splendor and back to play with me. But I never said a thing and was happy to let things stay as they were. I needed lots of things from life—a flood, a glut of things—but surely not more complications.

Anyway, as I was saying before I got distracted with my sexual fantasies and aren't old sexual fantasies always the best, my sweet noodle was standing there in her dress paging through a magazine and after a while she even looked up to me and held it up to indicate she wanted to buy it. I almost began to laugh; then I shrugged her off, gesturing that we didn't have enough for it, that we had hardly a dime to spare, which was true. Though I would have said so even if it wasn't the case, as the magazine was about the last thing in the world she needed. Glamour. Like she needed to look good lying in bed all day watching TV, or sometimes reading. Now let's be fair, she'd read books from the library, usually some sort of start-your-own-business-and-make-a-mint kind of books, though she couldn't hold a job, of course. If we're going to be fair, let's be really fair.

So my little doll was standing there, all squinty-eyed, her tousled head bent towards the glossy pages, with god knows what perverse thoughts looping about in her wayward bean. I was about five feet away from her (halfway between the magazine rack and the check-out) and every second getting more and more angry for making me wait, for pretending she had her shit together, and for everything, for lots of everything that I don't even want to get into again (but here I go). Finally, I said to her quietly, "Let's go."

"In a minute," she told me.

I stared at her for a minute—an hour—with an intensity that would have disintegrated most starlets, but she was immune to it by this point, so I said it again, "Let's go."

"Just a second," she said, and as she did she shot me a dirty, pitiful, vacant look, a nearly impossible chore for most, I know. But trust me, she had the puss for it, she had the chops. I began inching backwards, ever so slowly until I was nearly there, and this led her finally to eek out a pouty little, "Hmpphh," cram the magazine back into the rack, and follow me to the register.

Now, no one else had checked out or even come into the store while we were there. Then just before we got into the checkout lane, a big biker guy—a bearded, leathery, salty dog type

—stomped in to the store in his blue jeans and boots to buy a six-pack of beer. He was hustling to get it bought before nine o'clock, the deadline for such purchases in Milwaukee, and he got into the lane right in front of us, two seconds in front of us, and put his beer down just in front of my Cheerios and milk and other goods.

Now this was just after the state of Wisconsin had legalized the lottery, and there was kind of a lottery craze going on. Everybody was mad for it. I'd seen reasonable sorts—educated men, college professors even—sitting in bars buying ten dollar rows of tickets, sitting and scratching them, and being happy if they came close to breaking even so they could buy ten dollars more.

Some people did win, I guess. There had to be some big winners to string the rest of the saps along, and in the places they sold the tickets they had Polaroid pictures of the winners displayed, their big smiling mugs with notations like: "Joe Blow won $50," and "Sally Mae won $200."

It seemed that everybody had the fever. Except me, of course, I was sitting it out, staying sensible, and also because I rarely had even a dollar to spare, and if I did, I'd spend it on a forty-ounce Meister Brau, which could be had at the liquor store for 89 cents. I spent a lot of nights that summer after work walking the neighborhood, just killing time before I had to go back home, and taking some of the edge off, you know. It was just enough for that, a forty-ounce and I could go home and sleep at least.

Anyway, I guess to mark the occasion of the lottery, and entice their customers, the little grocery store was giving away free lottery tickets. Not the official State of Wisconsin ones, but their own brand, I think they must have been in it with a bunch of stores across the state; I don't know who was footing the bill for printing the tickets, probably Grocers of Wisconsin or something like that. And as far as I could tell, printing costs were about the only expense for the endeavor because all the tickets I'd seen said, "Sorry, try again," and winners were to the tune of "10% off your next loaf of bread" or "Half off a dozen eggs." This was the extent of it, but still it seemed everybody liked scratching the tickets, because in the garbage cans leading outside there were always hundreds of tickets scratched clean and even I liked scratching them.

So, as I was explaining, this guy paid for his beer and got his change and his free lottery ticket and he decided to scratch it off right there, right in line, on the little platform set up for writing checks.

As our few items were being rung up, I was watching him out of the corner of one eye, rubbing away on the ticket with a nickel that was nearly completely swallowed up with his big, dirty fingertips, and at the same time, I was watching the register total with each scan and looking down at the money in my hand, double-checking that I had enough, that the figuring I'd done as I'd been walking up and down the aisles had been correct.

Well, as soon as I was all rung up, twelve dollars and some cents (perfectly budgeted once again), this guy stood up straight, fast, like he'd been shot in the ass or something. He began to holler and whoop and shake his big arms and holler some more, just making noises at first—nothing intelligible.

I thought to myself, what in hell is going on, and even backed away a little from him as I was scared he had maybe picked this point in time to fall off his rocker. That would have been just my luck again. He was shifting his weight from boot to boot, like a squirmy little kid who had to go, making a clunking sound on the old tile floor. It was a good ten or fifteen seconds of this before he regained himself enough to let out his first discernible word: "Whoa!" and I realized he wasn't hurt or gone crazy, but happy somehow.

He shoved the ticket in the face of the cashier, who was, as it is, a special person (you know, not altogether there, not altogether on the mark). But she was from the family that owned the store, I think, and could handle the register all right. She was actually a champ at the register, punching the keys, scanning the goods, bagging things up, making change. She could do it all and was lucky, I suppose, to be born into a family where these skills were held in high regard.

But, when this guy held the ticket in her face, she just got kind of a blank look all over her (she was a champ at that too), and then the guy, still shouting and whooping it up, though in a more controlled manner, shoved the ticket in my face and screamed at me that he had just scratched off a winner to the tune of five thousand dollars. "FIVE THOUSAND BUCKS!" he howled, and I saw the $5,000 showing through the silvery film he had scratched away, and I heard myself say, "Damn."

He took a step towards me, like he was going to hug me or something, but then he stopped, because he couldn't hug me. Five thousand or not, he was still a tough guy on a beer run and I was a college busboy buying Cheerios. But he had to hug somebody, and he eyed my little sugar pie standing behind me, still in a huff by the way about not getting her magazine, and he showed her the ticket and she squealed, "Hooray for you!" like the cheerleader she'd been, and maybe if I hadn't seen here in that skirt all those years before when I'd been impressionable and liked the way she'd sashayed with those legs, well, maybe I could have avoided all this trouble in my life, but...

He brushed past me, reached out and hugged her and the two of them were all shrieks and smiles like it was New Year's Eve, the greatest party of all time. He may have even leaned in and planted one on her cheek, I don't know, but then he stepped back past me. As he did, he put out his hand out for me to shake, and I did, but he pulled away before I could give a good squeeze, a handshake representative of the person I really was.

Before I knew it, he was shouting it loudly again, "FIVE THOUSAND BUCKS!" nearly shaking the day's few remaining donuts lined up in the glass rack behind the register, and while this roar was still reverberating around us, he bowed his head and said quietly, almost reverently, like he'd just realized his goofy kid brother was the Second Coming or something, "Ho-ly shit."

It was about this time that the checker finally caught on to what was happening, and an aww-shucks excited glow filled in the blank on her face, and she said to him that she had not seen anything more than a two-dollar winner, and then began to get a little nervous about paying out. I could almost hear her brain go to work: Did she have to hand over the cash to him right then? Of course, she didn't have that kind of dough in the register.

"Five thousand?" she asked. "Are you sure?" He showed her the ticket again, and she nodded, yep, then the two of them just stood there smiling at each other, not sure what to do next.

It was at this point I finally took a good long look down at my little daisy standing behind me, and I just looked at her and looked at her and looked at her. I didn't have to tell her, like I don't have to tell you, that if we had just come in and got our stuff and checked out like the reasonable people we were purporting to be, we would have had that five thousand.

Five thousand dollars, now that was a lot of scratch. I don't mean to bellyache, but I would work five nights a week carting and cleaning dishes at the Big Boy restaurant downtown for, on a good night, six bucks an hour and that was about all we had to go on.

Sometimes she'd call her mom and cry on the phone and she'd come and take us on a grocery run or slip a twenty, to me usually, but we were running a pretty lean operation and all I could think as I stared down at her was, Damn. Damn. Damn. Damn.

When her head began to tilt up towards me, I turned and sighed and slapped over the cash for our groceries. The cashier made change and handed me my free lottery ticket. I grabbed it, groaned, picked up my groceries, and walked outside.

So there we were, me and my doll on the sidewalk outside of the store. I had the bag of groceries in my right hand, the ticket in my left with the gallon of milk, and as we walked slowly on the sidewalk in front of the store, I slipped the grocery bag handle around my wrist, brought my hands together close to my face, and in the light coming through the tall store windows, with my fingernail I scratched it off, our ticket. Of course it was a zilcher, a zero, a zip, nada, nothing, naught, the old goose egg, the old sorry try again, the old some fools never learn, the same old story, the same old same old, and I slipped it in the bag and chided myself for thinking for even one second, for half a second, that it could have been something else.

We shuffled home past the dirty apartment buildings full of neighbors we'd never know, past the liquor store where the lights were being turned off, and I tell you, those were three long blocks that night. About halfway home, my little lovely, my darling, the love of my life, asked me if she could help carry the load, and I said to her, "No." I said that I was even, that the weight was evenly distributed, and I was better off that way. Though really the handles of the plastic bag were cutting into the skin of one hand and the other was turning icy cold from the milk and it would have been a relief to hand something to her. But I said no because I was actually welcoming it—the pain, my suffering, my bad luck. I knew everybody needed something in life to depend on at least and that's what I had then.

We made it home to our shabby little building, trudged up the stairs, navigated the dark hallways to our door and once inside I put our few groceries away in the little kitchen. I poured myself a bowl of Cheerios and went to sit on the bed. That's all we had for furniture in there, all we could fit. And then my little turtledove flipped on the TV and knelt on the floor, turning through the channels. She went around the dial twice before stopping to ask, "Is this good?" I didn't even look, just let out a groan to let her know it was fine.

The Song of Solomon
Michael Joll

All Faith wanted was to be slim and pretty like Alice, and to have at least one friend. For as long as she could remember, Faith had toiled in Alice's shadow.

At the Stella Second School on Amherst Island, Faith worked diligently at her lessons, sat still at her desk, and spoke to her teacher, Miss Drummond, with respect. "Faith is well above average," Miss Drummond told Mrs. McGonigal at the end of Grade Seven. "She could easily complete High School, and even go on to become a teacher."

On receiving this news, Faith shrugged, much as her mother had. It was not normal for a son or daughter of an ordinary working man on Amherst Island to go beyond Grade Eight. Girls like her, Faith knew, spent the years between school and motherhood in service, or in a shop, or in one of the Island cheese factories.

*

The smell of cheese, of curdled milk and whey, had run through the McGonigal house all Faith's life. Her mother had worked at the cheese factory since long before the birth of either child. Alice had worked there since finishing school, and Faith knew that unless she went to high school, the smell would be on her too. And regardless of what Miss Drummond had said, high school was out of the question. She would have to work to help pay her way until such time as she married.

Faith's father, Albert, a man who'd come by his reputation as a drinker honestly, scraped a living as a harness maker and saddler. Drunk or sober, he ranted and raged at his lot in life, and blamed his wife and daughters for his poverty. The fact that her mother feared him was obvious to Faith, and for their parts, she and Alice feared him too. But Faith realized their mother had no escape from her life of drudgery and sour milk, and that her parents stayed together out of necessity. Like Alice, Faith knew she would probably end up like their mother unless she found the means to escape the path preordained for her—the cheese factory, a husband, children, and regular beatings.

On the last Sunday in August, Faith sat in a pew four rows back from the altar rail with her mother and Alice. She glanced at her sister whom, she noted, stared with rapt attention at the back of the minister's son, Noel McGuinness, who occupied the front pew with his mother. She's sweet on Noel, Faith thought, not that he's much to look at, but at least he's in high school. Bored with the sermon, Faith picked up her Bible and thumbed the pages. In Ezekiel, Chapter 16, Verse 14, she found the passage she sought: "As is the mother, so is her daughter." I am going to prove Mr. Ezekiel wrong, she told herself, starting today, and sat back with a smug look of determination on her face.

After the service, the three walked the dusty mile back to Stella in silence. Faith pushed the garden gate of their house on the Stella Forty Foot Road, held it open for her mother and Alice, and smiled at the thought that today was the first day of her new life. Upstairs, in the attic bedroom she shared with Alice, she took off her Sunday best dress and stood before the full length mirror, inspecting herself. She bounced on her heels. Her rolls of fat jiggled. Alice was never like this, she thought. She was always slim. And she had shape before she was my age. Even if I lose thirty pounds, I still won't be as slim as Alice. It's not fair.

Faith leaned forward and smiled into the mirror. Her crooked teeth smiled back. "There's nothing I can do about them," she muttered, and practiced smiling with a closed mouth. "And there's nothing I can do about my glasses." She went downstairs into the parlour, took a pair of shears from her mother's sewing basket, and returned to her room. In front of the mirror she cut off the pigtails that had been with her since she was three, and trimmed the rest of her hair to match her new, short bob cut.

Mrs. McGonigal shrieked when she saw Faith's new look. "I'm telling your father," she screamed. "You'll get a good hiding for this."

"He's in the Dominion Hotel, as I'm sure you know, mother," Faith said in an even tone. "Would you like me to fetch him, if he's not too busy?"

Faith's mother lunged at her. Faith sidestepped the wild swing and left her mother doubled over the kitchen table, sobbing. She glanced at the hall clock. Her father would be home for supper in four hours, when she would receive the hiding of her life. She knew what she had to do, and who would have what she needed: Maud McQueen, who sat next to her in class. The two were outcasts—Faith because she was plain and chubby, and Maud because she was the only Roman Catholic in the school.

Unlike most Amherst Islanders, Ulster Protestants who hailed from the rural Ards Peninsula on the Irish Sea, in addition to being Catholics, the McQueens were city folk, from Belfast, and therefore not to be trusted on either count. Alice had warned Faith that Maud, being a Catholic, would know about SIN. Particularly ORIGINAL SIN, and that she should be careful about being friendly with a dirty Papist. Faith was afraid to admit that she didn't know what original sin was, and didn't know any Papists, dirty or otherwise.

*

Maud was home when Faith called. In the shade of the front porch Faith whispered her needs.

"Yes, I can," Maud said. "Shall we do it together? It'll be such a lark."

Faith nodded. Maud ducked inside the house and appeared a couple of minutes later clutching two bottles. "No glasses," she said. "We'll take our medicine like men, straight from the bottle." They giggled. "Beer, a full pint, and a bottle of elderberry wine my mother made."

"Where?" Faith asked. "Are your parents at home?"

Maud nodded and put a finger to her lips. "Shh!"

"In back of Nielson's general store, then," Faith whispered. "No one will see us." They crossed the dusty road and slipped into the wooded shade behind the closed store.

"I know how to open a beer bottle," Faith said, pushing the twist of metal up and away from the neck. "I've seen my dad do it."

"Me too," said Maud. "You're the one in need. You go first."

Faith put the bottle to her lips and tipped it back. The froth burst out over her face and spurted down the front of her frock, leaving a large wet patch on her chest.

"Try that again, only slowly." Faith tipped the bottle back slowly, took a mouthful and passed it to Maud.

"I bet you don't know this," Maud said after taking her swig.

"What?"

"We have a different Bible from you Protestants."

"Never! There's only one Bible."

"Not true. The Catholic Bible has everything yours has and several other books too. They're at the end of the Old Testament in something called the Hypocrisy. And some of them have some really saucy bits in them."

"Such as...?"

"The Song of Solomon, for one."

"We have that."

"Bet you haven't read it, though."

"No," Faith confessed. "And I don't remember it ever being read in church."

"You wouldn't. It's all about sex."

Faith frowned. "What's that?"

"You know, what men and women do when they're married. And sometimes when they're not." Maud nudged Faith.

"How do you know?" Faith stammered, red-faced.

"I've read some of it. And my sister's nineteen and engaged, and she knows. She told me."

"I don't believe you."

"It's true. Read it for yourself. And Ecclesiasticus. I know you don't have that one in your Bible."

Faith stared open-mouthed.

"And Ecclesiastes. They don't read that in church either."

"How do you know so much about this sex stuff?"

"You mean to say your mother hasn't told you anything?"

"About what?"

"The birds and bees."

"What about the birds and bees?"

Maud shot her a disbelieving look and stuck her hands on her hips. "About how birds make more birds and how bees make more bees, and the same for cattle and dogs and people. Honestly, Faith, you really don't know much about what goes on outside school and church, do you?"

Faith scuffed her dusty shoes. "No, I guess not," she said in a small, quiet voice.

"Cheer up," Maud said. "How about I lend you my Bible and you can read all the bits they don't want you to read."

Faith perked up. "Don't tell anyone, Maud. You know how rotten grown-ups can be."

"Promise. I'll get it for you when we've finished drinking. Bring it back first day of school." Maud handed the beer bottle back to Faith.

"I don't like it much," Faith said, finishing the beer, "but I could get used to it, I suppose."

"If it acts like ether it won't matter. All that counts is you don't feel a thing when your father takes the strap to you."

Maud pulled the cork from the bottle of elderberry wine, put it to her lips, tipped it back, and drank. "That's nicer," she said, wiping her mouth with the back of her hand. "Try some."

Over the next hour they took turns drinking from the bottle until it was empty and their speech slurred.

"Friends forever, Faith," Maud said.

It was the first time anyone had mentioned being her friend. "Friends forever, Maud." She lay back and the clouds began to spin. She gripped the trunk of a sapling to prevent the world from turning over and throwing her into the vortex of the whirling pit. She rolled over onto her stomach, and threw up. She heard Maud do the same an arm's length away, muttering, "Oh, sweet Jesus," over and over again before they both passed out.

*

The sun was well down behind Nielson's general store before the two girls woke with pounding headaches and a sick sensation in their stomachs.

"We're going to be late for supper," Faith said.

Maud groaned. "I'll probably get a walloping from my father," she said, sitting up and pulling her frock over her knees.

"Me too," said Faith. "And one for cutting my hair. We might as well get it over with."

They staggered to their feet, pulled themselves up the bank of undergrowth and onto the road.

"Tell me about it tomorrow, Faith," Maud said as they parted company. Faith nodded and regretted even that small movement as the world spun then seemed to tip upside down.

"Where have you been all afternoon?" her mother screamed when Faith came in the front door. "Look at you. You've ruined your frock with grass stains, and goodness knows what you've got down the front. It looks like you've been sick."

Faith's father came in from the parlour and took one look at his daughter. "You're drunk," he said.

"So are you!" she shot back, slurring her words and rocking on her heels.

He tipped his head back and roared with laughter. "None of mine, I hope."

Faith shook her head and wished she hadn't.

"I wondered how long it would be before one of you tried it. Would you like another?"

"No," she replied in a tiny voice that did not seem to belong to her.

"Just look at what she's done to her hair," her mother wailed.

Albert McGonigal studied his daughter for a moment. "It's high time you cut those ridiculous pigtails off. They're for little girls. They look stupid on a young woman like you. For 50 cents it's nothing Mrs. McAusland can't put right in half an hour." He turned to his wife. "Now be quiet, woman, and fetch my supper."

Faith looked at her mother. "I don't think I shall have any supper tonight, mother," she said. "I'm on a fast." She turned and pulled herself by the handrail up the flight of steep, narrow stairs, stripped off her clothes in her bedroom and washed the sourness from her chest with the water from the bowl on the night stand. She slipped her nightdress over her head and lay down on her side of the bed, doubled over with dry heaves.

She fell asleep promising herself, "Never again."

*

The fast lasted until Tuesday when Faith felt almost normal again.

"Are you coming down today," her mother called up the stairs. "Or is God still punishing you for your foolishness and wickedness?"

"I have repented, mother, and God has forgiven me, so he says."

Alice put the finishing touches to her hair and turned away from the mirror. "Serves you right, you silly little ass," she said. "I'm surprised father didn't take the strap to you. You certainly had it coming."

Faith shot her sister a nasty look. "That's all well and good for you to say, Miss Goody-Two-Shoes, but I've decided to change how I live my life. So there!" She stuck her tongue out.

Alice turned away and lowered her head. "I've learned to stay out of his way, and when I can't, I do as I'm told. If you had any sense you would too." She looked up at Faith. "If you cross him you'll get what's coming to you whether you deserve it or not. I've tried. It doesn't work."

When she came down for breakfast, Faith saw the red welt on her mother's face. Her mother turned away, and mumbled, "Breakfast is on the table."

Alice shot her sister an 'I told you so' look, and ate her breakfast in sullen silence.

"I've decided I'm going to go to high school after this year," Faith announced. "I'm not going to work in the cheese factory. I'm going to become a schoolteacher. And I'm going to read the Bible every day for a year."

"That last bit's the first sensible thing you've said this morning, but I think your father may have other ideas about becoming a teacher. We need the money you'll bring in."

"It will keep father in beer," Faith retorted.

Her mother whipped round and slapped Faith's face. "He's a caring man," she hissed. Her hand touched the bruise on her face even as she said it. "Deep down, he loves us all." She turned her back on Faith and busied herself at the stove.

Faith looked at Alice, but her sister only stared at her bread and jam. She pushed the plate aside without finishing. "I'm off to work," she said as she slunk out the front door. Faith shrugged. Something, she could tell, was going on between her mother and Alice. Maybe they had had a fight. She decided to ask Alice that night before they fell asleep.

When Faith finished her chores she sat on the swing in the back yard, opened her Bible at the Song of Solomon, and read. By lunchtime she had finished and started reading it again. By tea time she had read it twice to make sure she had not missed anything the first time round. She finished reading it for the third time between tea and supper, and read Ecclesiastes for good measure by candle light in her bedroom with Alice sleeping beside her in the bed. Alice had refused to confide.

Ecclesiastes, she thought as she closed her Bible for the day, was not up to the same standard as the Song of Solomon, and that wasn't saying much. It was time, she decided, to borrow Maud's Catholic Bible and start Ecclesiasticus.

Faith looked over at Alice. I'm going to be slim like her one day soon. She blew out the candle and lay on her back with images from the Song of Solomon swirling around in her head. But the Song of Solomon really isn't that helpful, she decided. It is the Bible, after all.

*

On the last night of the summer holidays, Faith took Maud's Douay Bible to bed, and by the light of her candle read the entire book of Ecclesiasticus. Her anticipation that Maud was right and that Ecclesiasticus was full of what she called "sex," evaporated into disappointment in the small hours. Bleary-eyed for her first day back at school, Faith slipped Maud's Bible back to her at morning recess.

"Well?" Maud whispered.

"Have you read any of it?"

"No," Maud admitted. "I was going on what my sister told me." She brightened. "I'll see what else I can get. I know where she keeps her secret things. Maybe she'll have some postcards or something. She's getting married in the spring. I'm sure she must know what to do by now." But her voice betrayed her doubt as it tailed off.

"I thought you said she knew, and that she'd told you. How would I know if you're telling me the truth?"

Maud shuffled her feet. "I don't know who else to ask. I'm not asking my mother, that's for sure."

"Me neither."

"Or Miss Drummond."

"Gag me."

"Looks like we may have to stay ignorant, at least for a little while longer. There's always the Song of Solomon."

"I've read it," Faith said. "Three times. But it still doesn't tell us much, does it?"

"No. You're right. I've read it once. I probably shouldn't have got my hopes up."

*

Long faces and hostile silence greeted Faith when she returned from school. Her mother and Alice sat at the kitchen table, dabbing at their eyes and noses with handkerchiefs.

"What's the matter?" Faith said.

"Never you mind!" her mother retorted.

"I'm pregnant," Alice announced abruptly, and burst into tears.

Faith's mouth gaped open. "But you're not married. How can...?"

"The same way everyone gets pregnant," her mother snapped, giving Faith a hard look. "I'm not going into it now. Alice refuses to name the father."

"He doesn't know, mother," Alice bawled. "And he's married. I don't want him getting into trouble."

"As if he hasn't got you into enough trouble already," her mother snorted. She turned to Faith. "The doctor is certain. There's only one thing for it. She'll have to go to Kingston before anyone finds out, and have the brat born there. There'll be no bastards living in this house." She turned back to Alice. "Maybe the father will marry you, or you'll find some man stupid enough to take on both you and the baby."

Faith began to cry. Maybe Alice had been reading the Song of Solomon with a boy and somehow... How else...? "Does father know?"

"Not yet," her mother said.

As soon as their father came home Faith heard the roars in the parlour followed by the laying on of the strap. She climbed the stairs to their bedroom, too afraid of her father's rage to stand by her sister. Alice came up shortly afterwards, crying, closed the door behind her, and leaned against it. Faith put her arm around her sister, but Alice pushed her away.

"I'm fourteen and I'm pregnant," she wailed. "It's not my fault. I couldn't help it. He wouldn't take 'no' from me. He forced himself on me."

Faith's hand leapt to her mouth.

Alice pulled her clothes off and slowly turned a circle in the cramped space between the bed and the mirror. Faith stared at the red welts across her sister's back and buttocks.

"I know what you're thinking. You can't tell from looking, so how do I know, right?" Alice had stopped crying. She gritted her teeth. "I'll tell you how I know."

When Alice finished, Faith looked at her wide-eyed and white-faced in the candlelight.

"The doctor did all that to you?" she gasped.

Alice nodded. "And there's no mistake. The baby's due at the beginning of March, and like mother said, she and I will take the ferry on Saturday afternoon and go to Kingston. I'll find a room and a job, and have the baby there."

"But surely people will know."

"No one on the Island will know except us. My life is ruined, and I'm being made to feel guilty and ashamed for it." She lay face down on the bed and wept.

*

On Saturday, Alice and their mother set off to catch the afternoon ferry to Kingston. Faith and Alice huddled together on the Government dock, holding hands, not looking at their grim-faced mother. Their father was nowhere to be seen. Just before Alice took the gangway to the passenger deck she turned to Faith and kissed her on the cheek. "Wish me luck," she whispered.

"Good luck, Alice. I love you. I'll see you again soon, I promise. And I'll stand up to father, even if he straps me for it."

Alice turned away with tears in her eyes. Faith watched her follow their mother up the gangway and disappear among the throng of passengers on the far side of the ferry. From the dock Faith watched Noel McGuinness fishing from a punt close to the shore. She wondered if Noel was the father. But he had paid no attention to Alice, hadn't waved, or even glanced at her. No, she decided on reflection, he couldn't be the father. Alice had said the father was already married.

The ferry pulled away and rounded Stella Point, its wake washing against the banks and the black coal smoke from the stack streaming behind. Faith turned and trudged the short distance along Front Road to the Stella Forty Foot Road and her home, feeling small and alone.

As dusk fell on Amherst Island, Faith pulled out the galvanized tin bath from the shed, placed it in the middle of the kitchen floor, and filled it with jugs of warm water from the stove. Even though her mother and Alice would not be at church tomorrow, and her father certainly wouldn't be, that was no excuse for not being clean and wholesome herself. Her Sunday best dress hung in the wardrobe, ready to be worn for a couple of hours. All that was left was to scrub the week's dirt from her body.

Relaxing for a few moments in the bath, her anger at the unfairness of Alice's predicament slowly diminished. She finished bathing, stood, and reached for her towel. Her father reached for it first. She shrieked, doubled over, trying to cover her nakedness with her arms and elbows.

"I'll dry you, Faith," he said, breathing beer fumes in her face.

She tried to snatch the towel from his hands, but he dangled it out of reach.

No," she sobbed in a small, desperate voice. "Please." She closed her eyes.

"It's perfectly normal. I didn't hurt Alice, and I won't hurt you, either. Not if you're a good girl and do as you're told."

Strive to connect...

"sitting on the roof pondering motion and gravity"

The Naming of Things

In Singapore
Michael Joll

Aubrey Greenwood looked forward to going home—and dreaded it.

In the brief evening twilight, Greenwood sheltered from the monsoon deluge beneath the bridge wing of the *S.S. Vollendam*, a tumbler of gin in one hand and a cigarette burning in an ebony and ivory holder in the other. The tramp steamer swung at anchor in the roads, idling away the hours in solitude, waiting for the rising tide to allow it to cross the harbour bar. To starboard, hidden from view behind the ship's bridge bulwark huddled the teeming squalor of Malacca. To port lay the cleanliness of the open sea and countless fishing boats riding the oily swell.

Greenwood finished his cigarette and swallowed the last of the gin. He knew it would take more than Dutch courage to go through with it, but the enforced idleness of the voyage back to Singapore had afforded ample time—perhaps too much time—to grapple with the problem that had gnawed at his innards all the time he was away: What to do about Richardson?

The real heart of the matter was that he knew he was falling for Richardson. And that would not do. He was not ready, he admitted, perhaps even psychologically unable to undertake a life-long commitment to anyone, man or woman, and Richardson represented commitment, a suffocating prison, and the mere thought of those walls left him breathless.

Richardson had to go.

He saw a rain squall approaching and headed for the dining saloon. At the Captain's table he took his place and acknowledged the passengers already seated. In the long periods of silence while they ate, his untethered mind floated to Richardson. The very thought of the man evoked visions of the brief but nasty scene to come; raised voices, finger pointing, accusations, and denials. He would sooner face a dentist's drill. 'Coward,' his inner voice mocked. He hid his trembling hands beneath the table. His stomach ulcer bit. He gritted his teeth until the spasm passed.

His cotton undershirt clung to his body like a wet sheet. A rivulet of sweat trickled from his temple, ran inside his collar, and soaked into his starched shirt. He knew it was not simply the humidity of the July air drifting in from the open porthole. He dabbed at the beads of perspiration with a silk handkerchief and tucked it back into the breast pocket of his linen jacket, but he could do nothing to rid the smell of fear leaching from his armpits. He glanced at his table companions. How had they failed to notice? He needed a drink to soothe his jitters but, as he had discovered on joining the ship at Rangoon, the *S.S. Vollendam* did not serve liquor with meals.

He excused himself from the dinner table as soon as good manners permitted, took with him a full tumbler of gin from the bar to deaden his nerves, and made his way onto the cargo deck. The rain had stopped. In its place, the cloying stench of fish, pork fat and boiled cabbage, syphoned from the galley by the ventilation funnel, hovered over him. He considered undoing his collar stud and loosening his necktie but decided against it. That would not be proper for an Englishman, not in front of the Dutch officers, and certainly not in front of the passengers. Instead, he eased a finger around the inside of his celluloid collar, loosening the noose around his neck for a moment.

He made his way upwind of the nauseating smell and leaned against the deck rail. From the slight breeze in his face, and the vibrating steel beneath his feet, he knew the boilers were making steam. The ship swung its stern to the land and the few dim lights that marked Malacca vanished as one behind a rain squall. Singapore and his adopted home, tomorrow night.

Before the squall hit, Greenwood hurried to his preferred spot under the bridge wing, taking shelter from the torrents spilling in ragged streamers from the scuppers overhead. He downed half the tumbler of gin in three gulps, conscious of the need to collect his thoughts and return a quick, final verdict on the Richardson matter before the alcohol fogged his brain.

Singapore. Richardson. He weighed both options.

In a Singapore without Richardson, divorced from the complication of any relationship except with his typewriter, he could gather the raw material he needed to build his stories. His writing, he allowed, was his passion, his obsession, and the only mistress to whom he owed and granted loyalty. Without Richardson's restraining anchor, he could mingle freely with Singapore's jostling throngs and linger in their bamboo and rattan-walled shops reeking of joss, where Hindu, Muslim, Chinaman, and Malay conducted their secretive business. And without Richardson he could trawl Singapore's clubs, bars and brothels, prowl its docks, wharves and godowns where, unnoticed, he observed the quirky individuals he transformed into the characters who breathed life into his novels.

Deep down however, he knew that when the salons of Southeast Asia, and the drunkards, whoremongers and louche lounge lizards like himself who frequented them no longer held appeal, like every other writer of his acquaintance, he would move on. In that respect, Singapore was temporary, like Richardson.

He turned his attention to Richardson, who was different from the other men and the occasional woman who had drifted through his life, all of them small pebbles whose splash had left scarcely a ripple on his broader sea. He knew he would miss the vulnerable, willowy pianist with the long, delicate fingers and the unfocused stare of shell-shock, but he would undoubtedly get over him in time.

The young man was, without doubt, talented but, Green-wood suspected, there would be no professional concert platform. He could guess what Richardson would do when he stopped deluding himself about a musical career. Only the method was in doubt: a quick, fashionable accident in the gun room of his parents' house, perhaps? Or a lingering suicide of alcohol and Burmese poppy milk as the poisons infused and destroyed his body and mind? The latter, more probably, for he had scant doubt that Richardson, like himself, lacked the moral fibre to do the proper thing, and always would.

Either way, by then Richardson would be gone and his fate no longer Greenwood's concern.

Weary of the discourse, he congratulated himself on his decision, but his ever-present, querulous companion, his nagging doubts, lingered.

*

Late the next night the *S.S. Vollendam* docked at Singapore. Greenwood made his way through stamp-wielding officialdom and took a motorcycle rickshaw through the tropical rain to Raffles Hotel. He had called his room in the hotel home for more than three years. The double bed, private bathroom and small balcony beyond the French doors suited his needs, providing a refuge for proper white men like himself, comfortable enough when the power was on.

True to form, on his arrival he discovered the power was out.

In bad humour, he groped his way around his writing desk in the dark, and undressed. Resigned to spending the night beneath the folds of the mosquito net alongside Richardson's hot body, he poured half a tumbler of gin, downed it in three gulps and slipped into the bed. But the alcohol proved neither soporific nor comforting. Quailing at the prospect of the coming morning's showdown, his mind whirled. Lying rigid in the airless, humid night, bathed in a sheen of sweat, sleep evaded him.

Drawn and haggard, Greenwood rose before dawn. The tepid bath water did nothing to improve his sour disposition. In semi-darkness, groomed, shaved, and dressed in a silk dressing gown wrapped over his shirt and trousers, he stepped out onto the balcony of his hotel room. While he watched the rain cleanse the city he fingered his cravat and fiddled with the sash of his dressing gown, shuffling his feet and twisting his body. He pushed a cigarette into his holder, but did not light it.

As the downpour blurred the outlines of the balconies of the rooms across the courtyard, he wondered for an anxious moment if he was viewing them through a muslin shroud: His own? Soon enough, he knew; but, please God, not yet. A shiver ran the course of his spine and left goosebumps. His ulcer reacted with an explosive spasm. He shut his eyes and tried to focus on how best to rid himself of Richardson.

Though afflicted by many vices, cheroot smoking did not number among them, so the pungent smell of Indonesian tobacco drifting into Greenwood's nostrils pried him from his bout of depression. A moment later, Richardson, dressed in a borrowed pair of Greenwood's pyjamas, appeared without a sound at his side, the evil-smelling cigarillo cupped between thumb and forefinger in his bony hand, the way soldiers used to do in the trenches in the war that had spared him, but not Richardson.

As a British secret agent in Switzerland for most of the war, ending with the armistice six years earlier, Greenwood had avoided exposure to heroics. Now, faced with the Richardson dilemma, he knew he had to make his final move that morning, before his nerve deserted him like it had that winter day in '17 in Montreux. The thought of taking decisive action pierced his body like a collector's pin through a moth. He regarded his white knuckles gripping the railing, and shuddered. Coming to grips with his most shameful, most loathsome affliction, he refiled the indelible memory of Montreux and swallowed the bile rising in his throat.

How to break the news? The guillotine; a swift, clean execution, forthright as man to man? Or a gentle let-down for fear of causing unnecessary pain to the sensitive young chap? Surely, after their months together, didn't Richardson deserve no less than a delicate disengagement? He prayed that Richardson could not see his knees shaking beneath his dressing gown, and turned to face him, as prepared as he would ever be to accept the consequences of his next words.

"Good morning, Aubrey," Richardson mumbled.

"Good morning, old man. Sleep well?"

"Not very well; no." Richardson threw his cigarillo over the balcony, then hid his hands behind his back as he laced his fingers together and untied them several times. He studied his bare feet as if seeing them for the first time. He drew a deep breath. "I don't quite know how to put this to you," he blurted out in a quavering voice. "But I have to leave. If I'm to resume my concert career I must return to England."

Greenwood opened his mouth to reply. "No," Richardson said, holding up a hand. "Please let me finish. My parents live in Sussex. They've plenty of room and a baby grand for me to practice on while I decide what I'm to do next. So you see, Aubrey, I can't stay in Singapore forever. I have to say 'Good-bye.' Today. Now. You do understand that, don't you?"

He turned to Greenwood, his face pleading and his eyes bright. He blinked several times. Tears tumbled down his cheeks. A nerve jigged beside his temple.

Lie, or truth? Either way, in an instant Richardson's explanation, like the man, no longer mattered. Richardson had unwittingly spared Greenwood the drama of a break-up.

"I'm sorry to hear that, my boy, truly sorry, but I certainly understand." Greenwood hoped that the lie carried conviction.

"You've been so kind to me, Aubrey..." Richardson's voice tailed off as more tears spilled down his cheeks.

"Say no more, dear boy," Greenwood said. "I shall cherish the memory of every minute that we spent together. I shall never forget you."

Without offering his hand, Greenwood turned his back on the young man, his knees quiet and his grip on the railing relaxed. "If you intend to leave today," he said, looking over his shoulder, "perhaps you should pack." He saw Richardson flinch and held his breath in case the young man's new-found resolve should crumble.

"Yes, of course. You're right." Richardson's voice remained strained. A slight swish of the silk dressing gown, and Richardson was gone from the balcony. Greenwood exhaled. He smoothed his brilliantined hair with a light touch then lit the cigarette in his holder, grateful that Richardson had not forced his hand or exposed the fear that lurked beneath his façade. He remained on the balcony, his back to the open French doors, careful to avoid any movement that Richardson might interpret as an attempt at reconciliation. A reversal of his good fortune at this critical moment would not do at all.

Greenwood heard the chink of glass and the gurgle of pouring liquor. He did not begrudge Richardson one last drink. He heard the hotel room door close with a soft click. In a few minutes Richardson would be out of the hotel and Greenwood could turn his attention to his beloved Underwood typewriter and resume his neglected livelihood.

He remained on the balcony, counting down the minutes to freedom. The rain stopped abruptly and he noticed the greenery in the large earthenware pots in the courtyard as if for the first time. His mood brightened. He turned away from the balcony, crossed the bedroom floor and stood by the bed they had shared all those months. The sheets lay rumpled, still warm to the touch. The smell of Richardson's night sweat lingered, mingling with the reek of his cheroot. A momentary pang of guilt at his callousness towards the young man touched a nerve, then quickly evaporated.

He sat at his writing desk and cracked his knuckles. It was time to write; past time. He pulled open a drawer and took out two sheets of paper. He reached into the other drawer where he kept his carbon paper and his old service revolver.

His fingers probed, then scrabbled for the hard steel. He broke into a cold sweat.

Richardson was gone—and the revolver with him.

The Naming of Things
Nancy Kay Clark

One day when I was ten and just beginning to understand my incredible powers, I asked a crow whether it was true all plants and animals had to obey me. He bowed his head yes. I smirked at him and like an idiot said, "Okay, I order two killer whales to beach themselves."

The crow blinked at me, nodded his head again, and flew off.

A week-and-a-half later, I heard on the radio that two perfectly healthy killer whales had beached themselves on Vancouver Island—to the great puzzlement of Canadian government scientists. No one could budge them, and despite a host of volunteers draping wet clothes on their backs around the clock, the whales baked to death in the sun.

Heart pounding, I ran out of the house and called for the crow. "Please, please tell me it was just a coincidence. I mean, how could two whales all the way out on the west coast know what I said?"

The crow blinked and replied, "The message was conveyed to them. I told a rat who was travelling on a train west that afternoon. When he arrived, he told a gull, who went and told two whales, who accepted their fate and immediately did your bidding."

"Holy shit!" I shouted, repeating one of my father's favourite expletives. From then on, I was very careful about what I ordered flora and fauna to do.

I grew up to be an exterminator—an environmentally friendly exterminator because I don't have to poison or trap anybody. I just ask them politely to leave and they do.

One night in August, I drove to Cabbagetown to clear some bats out of an attic. It was a three-storey Victorian, scheduled for massive renos. A metal dumpster had already been delivered—ready to receive the onslaught of reno debris. It squatted on the front lawn, crushing the grass and dandelions who whispered their pain to me as I walked by. The owners, my clients, weren't there; they hadn't moved in yet. I got the key out of the lock box, opened the door and made my way up to the attic. As I entered through the trap door stairs, I was immediately swamped by sensations—the attic was buzzing with talk. I bowed low, as a dozen mice came to greet me. "Good evening. Sorry to disturb you," I said.

They bowed back and launched into complaints about their neighbours—the bothersome dust mites in the old sofa, the centipedes who steal their food, the incessant buzz of the flies in the windowsills. They demanded that I do something about it—as if I were Mother Nature's landlord. I said something non-committal, but I warned them that if they didn't like noise they should really move out because their home was about to become a construction zone. Then I asked them where the bats were. They directed me to a spot near the chimney.

It was a small maternal roost, probably twenty bats in total, all mothers and babies. They were sleeping. At dusk, the mothers, babies clinging to their bellies, would wake and fly out of the hole in the rafters to spend the dark night hunting. I stood and watched them for a while—though some were stirring, they seemed so peaceful—but soon, as it always happens, I became aware of the thousands of lice humming, feeding, crawling through the bats' fur. They made such a racket—it gave me a headache. So I went over to a window, pried it open, and squeezed through it to sit on the slanting roof and wait for dusk. There was no need to wake the bats so early. Let them dream.

I felt myself relax as I surveyed my dominion. A slight breeze had cooled the sticky air of the afternoon. In the west, the low red sun sent streaks of pink overhead through the contrails the jet planes made. The swifts skittered across the sky, catching mosquitoes on the wing. The silver maple in the backyard creaked with old age; its black squirrels scrambled over it, ignoring its complaints. It was August and the time of year that Monarch butterflies gather before going south. A whole bunch of them, bouncing in the breeze, loped by the roof. I caught snatches of excited and frightened voices. "Where are we going? Does anyone know? How long will it take us?" They talked about the journey ahead of them—a journey that none had ever taken before, but which was etched into their DNA, felt in their tissues. And I wondered—not for the first time—about the ancestor I was named after, the first Adam, and how he came to name things.

Fritillary and Snow Leopard. Platypus and Newt. Sanderling and Macaroni Penguin. Bloodroot and Acacia. I love the feel of these names on my tongue. How did he think them up? Did he settle on some scientific, logical method, or was it pure whimsy? I'm not talking about the Latin species names, the science of taxonomy—but the original names Adam bestowed. Of course, he was not speaking English, but some proto-Indo-European/Uralic/Afro/pan-world tongue. I imagine in my mind Adam creating language as he uttered the sounds and named the world for the first time. God may have created the universe, but Adam named everything in it and, in doing so, cranked the key and set it all in motion.

I was sitting on the roof pondering motion and gravity, when I heard a cry. It came from my left. I half crawled, half slid over to look. It was a bird—a mourning dove. He had a sharp, thin black beak and a long tail. His back and tail were blue grey. His breast was rusty. Panting heavily, he lay on his side, a crushed wing beneath him. A bloody gash stained his belly feathers brown-red.

"What happened?" I asked.

"Damn cat. I barely made it up here," the bird muttered— then I think he fainted from pain. I should have left him then and there, but I was curious. I settled down beside him and stroked the feathers on his head. A minute or two later, the bird revived.

"Help me!" he pleaded.

I sighed and put my head down on the shingles—so that we could talk eye to eye. "I can't. I'm sorry. I have a strict policy. If I help you I have to help everyone and there's not enough hours in the day, not enough days in the week to do that. I don't have enough resources (well, money really, but try explaining the concept of money to a dying bird). I don't have enough knowledge."

"But you are Adam. You can speak to us..."

"Yes, but I don't have the power to save you. I'm sorry."

"You could tell the cats not to attack us."

This was an argument I had heard before. "So I'm going to tell them they can't eat? That they have to starve to death?"

He huffed and rolled his black eye, as if to say, "Oh, come on, like cats actually eat everything they hunt? Their humans feed them."

True—but the principle remained. "Sorry, I can't."

"You could tell them only to hunt the old. I'm young. I have yet to mate." Birds don't shed tears—but if they could I knew this bird would be sobbing now. I could hear it in his voice.

I felt so stupid lying there shrugging, saying over and over again. "I'm sorry, no." But what else could I do?

"You could ask for bird volunteers. Those who were too sick or old could volunteer to be eaten," he said.

And I thought, Christ, yeah, that'll work. I mean, no one ever thinks they're too old to live. He stopped talking. I rolled onto my back and looked up. The pink tendrils in the sky had vanished beneath a swathe of deepening grey. The streetlights had just come on and through their haze, I could see two of the stars in the Summer Triangle. "I have to go. I have business with some bats."

"Don't. At least sit with me a while."

I rolled back on my side to look at him and settled there, knowing that I'd probably miss my opportunity to speak with the grandmother bat. I asked the bird: "Are you from around here?

He didn't know. He had vague flashes of memory—a warm nest, the bright feathers of his mother, a little grove of trees dotted with nests, the chatter of his extended family, sunlight, the blue sky. And then for the longest time he lived in a black box dotted with breathing holes—and the only thing he saw were the human hands that fed and watered him. And then he described a whole series of cages, the last of which had been placed in the backyard of a house. Through human error, the cage door had not been properly shut. He flew. He could not tell me how long ago that was, but said that he had spent his time since dodging foxes and cats and hawks, looking for that grove of trees. He'd never found it.

He took an hour to die—the reds and blues of his feathers fading under the night sky, until he looked indistinct. I picked his body up and contemplated giving it to a passing owl—no point in letting it go to waste, but at the last moment I didn't. I picked him up; he left a dark spot where his blood had stained the roof shingles. I whispered his first name, which he had told me just before the end. I won't repeat it; it's practically unpronounceable in English anyways.

I went back through the attic window, slipped his body into a plastic bag and put it in my backpack. The bats had gone out for the night, so I'd have to catch them as they returned. I settled on the old sofa, cozying up to the mites, to wait for dawn.

Delusional Date
Phyllis Humby

Rafe:

Bloated mosquitoes buzzed at my neck. With one slap I smeared their blood into the gritty dirt around my shirt collar. Stepping off the back porch, I headed to the crick just beyond the grain shed. Not a breath of air, even at night. Another long, dry summer.

Though the dust near choked me working at ole Brubacher's, I liked the jingle of money in my pocket. Rock pickin' was done and I saved every cent. Well, 'cept for that model car from the drug store. It was a beaut. And, yeah, the chewin' tobacco. Darned near made me puke. Glad my brother Ned didn't know 'bout that.

The full moon lit up the crick as I stepped out onto the felled tree trunk. After peeling off my shirt, I dropped my pants and slid into the murky water.

I was thinkin' 'bout going into town on Saturday. Thinking of asking that fat girl from church to go to the pictures with me. Cindy's her name.

My brother Ned has a girl, Laura. She always wears that same old cotton dress. The one that buttons all the way down the front. It's kind of a faded blue with little flowers on it. When she walks past, I can smell somethin' sweet an' nice, like the wild jasmine that grows along the ditch past Ruker's place. She's quiet like. Laura acts shy, but Ned says she ain't shy with him.

One day I asked my brother if she let him go all the way. He put his palm against my forehead and pushed me backwards into the tractor. He smiled, and then threw back his head laughing, like it was Friday night or somethin'. "Gentlemen never tell, jughead."

Just thinking 'bout Laura made me wish I had somebody just like her.

Childish girls dog me when I'm in town. Wait for me outside the general store and then giggle and run when I come out. My mom says I attract them like June bugs to a screen door. The silly ones. Skittish, my dad calls them. The older ones, the real pretty ones, don't even see me.

Taking a deep breath, I dunked my head under the water and came up with my wet hair plastered to my face. Climbing back onto the tree trunk, I shook myself like a big ole long-haired dog, and stepped back into my dusty pants. I tugged my boots on and swung my shirt over my shoulder. Whistling, I strolled back to the house, my mind fixed on taking that church girl to the pictures. A guy's gotta start somewhere.

Cindy:

At first, I couldn't believe my ears when Rafe invited me to the pictures. I could barely speak. Even Momma admits he is the most handsome boy in the whole town with his blond hair and blue eyes. He always wears a scowl on his face, like he's in serious thought, or just mad at the whole world. When I see that look my stomach feels all quivery.

I was afraid Momma and Daddy wouldn't let me go. Then Daddy had to go to the city for a couple of days with Gramps, and Momma said she forgot to mention it before they left. Gran smiled, saying that I was growing up way too fast for her.

Momma fretted about me meeting a boy without a chaperone, and wanted to send my older brother Jacob along. I just about died at the thought, and when she saw me so frantic, she promised not to tell Jacob, or any of my other brothers and sisters. They would give me no peace if they knew.

Rafe:

On Saturday, I washed up, and took my good shirt from the hook. The sleeves were shorter than when I'd last worn it. With a shrug I left the house, the screen door slamming like the crack of a gun.

Ned was waiting out front in the truck. After he dropped me off in town, I could hear his laugh as he shifted gears and chugged up the dirt road.

When I'd mentioned the picture show to Cindy, she'd rolled her eyes. Just when I thought I couldn't hold my breath no longer, she said yes. It made me mad thinking about how long she took to give me an answer.

When I saw her waiting by the picture house she was wearing a damn hat, like she was my mother or something. I inched back to the corner of the building. She noticed me and waved. Then she tugged at her hat until it slid into her hand and disappeared behind her back.

I shoved my fists deep into my pockets and fingered the heavy silver coins. My jaw set, I hunkered towards her. I was getting a headache from frownin' so hard, but my face felt like stone and there weren't nothing I could change about that.

Cindy had a big grin on her stupid face. I could see her buckteeth. At least she'd got rid of the hat.

Cindy:

On Saturday, I hung my Sunday dress on the back of the door, and commenced to getting ready. I washed my hair in rainwater until it squeaked, and then using the basin in my room, scrubbed from head to toe. Gran gave me a bit of lavender oil to add to the water.

Wearing only my petticoat, I laid on my bed trying to stay cool until it was time to leave. Momma entered my room with a cotton print dress that I recognized, draped over her arm. She said she never got to wear it much anyhow and it would be much prettier on me. Even with alterations, it fit me a tad snug. Baby fat, Momma called it.

She then presented a hat. An old one of hers that she had fussed over. "You can't go into town to meet a boy without dressin' proper." Afraid to hurt Momma's feelings, I told her it looked real fine.

The youngsters scrambled across the room when they saw me dressed up. Momma distracted them with a promise of homemade ice cream. Thankfully, Jacob was nowhere to be seen.

The picture show was within walking distance of our house. Crossing the dirt-packed road, a layer of gritty sand settled on my shoes. Feeling clammy, I slowed my step, worried that the moisture would seep through the thin cotton of my dress.

I watched as Ned dropped Rafe off down the road. He seemed to hesitate, like he had forgotten something. My stomach fluttered and my legs felt weak and wobbly. I smiled and waved. Feeling self-conscious in Momma's hat, I slid it off my head.

Rafe:
Dust covered my boots and pants as I scuffed up onto the boardwalk. "Yeah, let's go in."

I made up my mind that I was leaving if she started to giggle. I knew I shouldn't be mad at her. I coulda asked somebody else to go with me but this being a first date an' all...

After paying admission, I sat down without saying a thing to her. She settled in the seat beside me and I could hear her breathing through her nose. Short, stuffy snorts, like ol' Peg back on the farm.

My knee jumped and jiggled in constant motion as I thrummed the armrest. Finally, I just grabbed Cindy's hand and jumped up out of the seat, practically dragging her behind me. "Let's just walk. It's a dumb movie anyhow."

If she said anything, I didn't hear it. She was skip-walking to keep up when I headed toward the river, cutting through the alley between the tavern and the hardware store—stepping around suspicious puddles in the hard dirt. My hands were clenched in my pockets and my face hurt from being all pinched up as I trudged through the tall grass behind the main street.

Cindy:
When Rafe reached the picture house, he sure didn't say much of a greeting. Before I knew it, we were sitting side by side. He acted real nervous, making

me wonder which one of us would be sick first. All of a sudden, we were both flying out of that picture show.

Once we were outside, Rafe let go of my hand, and headed towards the river. I had to pretty much run to keep up. When he sat on the ground, I hesitated, knowing I could soil my dress, and wondering what Momma would say if I did. Slowly, I sank to the dirt.

He didn't look at me, or talk to me, or do much of anything. I thought that maybe all boys acted this strange.

Rafe:

At the diseased elm tree, I slid to the ground. Tugging a long, dry stalk out of the dirt, I stuck it between my teeth and watched the green water inch forward along the bank.

Cindy hesitated, and then like an old arthritic hound, she lowered her short, stocky body to the grass-patched dirt. Her black laced shoes reminded me of the grey-haired schoolteacher, Miss Mills.

Not able to wait one more minute, I spoke my mind. "Shoot, are you gonna let me kiss you, cuz if you ain't, I got lots o' work I could be doing."

Her eyes widened, like she was excited, and then she nodded her head.

Cindy:

Rafe looked so handsome chewing on that old straw, I coulda just died. When he asked about kissing me, all I could think was, I'm sure glad Jacob's not here.

A strand of Rafe's hair had fallen over his eyes. My heart pounded when he looked at me. I knew that if I didn't kiss him, I would regret it every day for the rest of my life, even if I lived to be a hundred.

Rafe:

I leaned forward, and then remembered the strand of grass. Grabbing it out of my mouth, I pressed my lips against an outcropping of teeth. After a few seconds, I pulled away from her. Seeing the stupid look on Cindy's face made me all the madder. Disappointed as all get out, I wondered why kissing was such a big deal.

Then she reached for the back of my head and gently pulled me forward. She pressed her mouth on mine, urging my lips apart, until I felt her tongue along the bottom of my teeth. My arms wrapped around her waist until her body was pressed so tight to mine that I couldn't breathe. I wished Ned could see me now. This was better than any old picture show.

Cindy:

When Rafe kissed me, it didn't seem right. My friends at school talked a lot about kissing. We'd practiced kissing each other when we were playing at Jenny McGregor's. One time, Jenny was up in a tree when her sister and boyfriend came along. She just about toppled out when Sue Ellen and Cal settled in at the base of the tree. Jenny learned a lot that day.

I decided to show Rafe what I knew about kissing. He liked it. He learned fast. Real fast. I have to admit, I liked it too. I'd never been held that tight before, and especially not by a boy—especially not by a boy like Rafe. I felt a fierce heat. My shoes were getting all dusty and my poor dress, well, I knew it would be a sight.

When I got home, Momma and the young ones were on the back porch. I could hear Gran calling to them from the vegetable garden. I hightailed it upstairs and changed my clothes. Throwing myself across the bed, I closed my eyes. My face was hot and flushed recalling the liberties Rafe had taken—the liberties that I had allowed. Rafe Jackson and I had fallen in love right then and there on the banks of the river. I just knew we'd be together forever.

Rafe:

My face ached from grinning the whole five miles back to the farm. I'd already decided who I'd ask to the pictures next Saturday. Pretty little Amy Watson that helped out at the general store.

Just in time for chores, I headed right to the barn. Ned was already milking when I strutted through the open doorway.

"What's that big grin all about, kid?"

"A gentleman never tells, Ned, a gentleman never tells."

300 Miles to Leadville

Frank T. Sikora

If Mother knew I had picked up a hitchhiker, she would have thrown a good old Southern tantrum—long stretches of self-suffering silence interspersed with even longer stretches of self-righteous rage. But Mother wasn't there, and I was lonely for conversation, someone to help occupy the last 300 miles to Leadville. Besides, he looked harmless enough. He was barely older than a boy, maybe nineteen, and oh so dreamy. In his fashionably worn T-shirt and tight jeans, with his dark eyes, curly brown hair, and sculpted form, he was like Michelangelo's David come to life, and I couldn't just leave him on the side of the highway. That would have been rude, and Mother always told me manners count even more than money. At times, she believed it.

I offered my prettiest smile. "Welcome aboard, I'm Maizy."

He didn't acknowledge me, not at all. He just climbed in and sat, improbably still and impossibly beautiful. I almost cast my last breath right there.

"That's Maizy with a 'z'," I said, "not an 's'. Yours?"

No response. He stared straight ahead, lost in the majesty of my bug-splattered windshield.

"All right, duly noted, but you'd better know I'm heading to Leadville. I'm delivering 600 pounds of ammonium nitrate to a group of End of Days Bible Beaters. I'm on a tight schedule. No stops. No diversions. Still game?"

He might have twitched.

"Look here," I said. "It's fine by me if you want to marinate in your autistic stew, but I feel like chatting. I have plenty of stories to tell, and some of them are even true." That's Mother's favorite joke. "Do we have an understanding?"

Apparently we did. Because without standing, he stripped down to God's essentials and then tossed his clothes out the window.

"Oh dear," I said, blushing a mighty rose. "I appreciate the gesture, but you're way too young for me to do anything but admire. And trust me. I do, oh, so admire."

He leaned back and lifted his feet onto the dashboard.

I took that as my signal to get moving and guided the van back onto the highway, exhaled, and proceeded to ramble on like an Oklahoma twister. I told him about my six years at Vassar and how I had managed to accumulate more than 130 credits, including forty in Art History, and not earn a degree. I told him how I had started my delivery business after school. At first it was legit, but the faltering economy forced me to accept less than legal packages. I told him that to save money I lived in the van. I showered at the YMCA and I banked online. I insisted that I liked the freedom, even the danger. For two hours, he listened to all this and more, including how I had not talked to Mother for nine years. I might have cried a bit, but he hung in there until I finished—all 150 miles' worth.

Then he flung himself out the door.

I was too astonished to yell or even stop until I had traveled another 100 yards. The van skidded to a noisy and oil choked halt. Empty boxes fell from the shelves. For a moment, I feared my cargo might somehow explode. I wasn't clear on the physics. After all, even with 130 credits at Vassar, I didn't take any real science courses.

I jumped out and sprinted back along the road's shoulder. I must have looked pathetic, stumbling hither and fro like some drunken sorority twit. I found no sign of the boy. Not a speck of torn flesh or a bloodstain.

I think I searched for a good forty minutes before I gave up and shuffled back to the van, not crying but close. I didn't understand what had happened to him. A boy just couldn't disappear, could he? Where did he go? It didn't make sense.

Two years later, it still doesn't. Sometimes, usually when I am tired or jazzed up on uppers trying to make my last delivery on time and under the radar, I look for him, hoping to see him standing at the edge of road, his long hair flowing, his perfectly chiseled face tilted toward the sun.

All I know is that for two hours the loveliest boy gracing God's earth had accompanied me. He listened to my stories, quietly, without judging, without condemning. He entered my van, a van carrying 600 pounds of shit to a group of righteous imbeciles, and reminded me there was beauty in the world. Even Mother would have approved.

With Regret

Michael Joll

Why does all the world love a rogue?

I don't have an answer. From hairpiece to corns we're all cut from the same bolt, and I should know. I'm a reprehensible bastard, for which I offer no apologies, and it's too late to change. I was not always thus, but the years in short pants do not count for much. I have deserved little of what I have acquired, either good or bad, during my one hundred and one years on this earth, and I don't pretend otherwise. I may be obscenely wealthy, little of it earned by the honest sweat of my brow, but I am no hypocrite, perhaps my only laudable trait.

I trace my downfall precisely to 1:45 p.m. on April 2, 1933, my twenty-first birthday, when I received a letter by special delivery. Inside the envelope I found a key which I did not recognize. The accompanying letter of explanation was from my Uncle Bertie, my guv'nor's older brother, dated the previous day. It read:

"Dear Percival,

Congratulations on turning twenty-one tomorrow, my boy. No doubt your parents will give you the key to the door with all due ceremony. The enclosed is the key to a new Rolls-Royce Phantom II drop-head coupé. Hyphen Motors in Park Lane will deliver the motor to you in Dorking tomorrow. I hope you will enjoy it for many years to come and remember me from time to time,

Your uncle,
Bertie"

I knew Uncle Bertie was rolling in boodle, but this was grand and unprecedented generosity. I reread the letter and took note of the date. Was this an April Fools' joke? I wasn't sure until three o'clock that afternoon when a pantechnicon pulled into my parents' driveway. Two supercilious, white-gloved and buff-coated men alighted, opened the rear door, and wheeled the car out and down the ramp onto the gravel drive. My verbal reaction was a single, unprintable word. Thus began my life-long affair with my favourite mistress, the car I named Anastasia.

On my way from Dorking back to Balliol to finish my final term, I dropped in on Uncle Bertie to grovel before the feet of the great man, my benefactor, and place myself forever in his service.

"The four door Phantom," Uncle Bertie announced gravely, "has a rear seat which can effectively be used for a purpose not originally contemplated by the designer, but I rather thought you would, on the whole, prefer the two-seater. It attracts a sportier sort of gal. And besides, a hotel offers more comfortable and spacious overnight accommodation for one's more energetic companions."

Many considered Uncle Bertie a bit of a rogue in his day, one who, even when well over sixty, rarely looked a gift horse in the mouth. But Uncle Bertie was childless, possibly on account of an incident involving an aggrieved husband and a polo mallet, so over the years he had come to regard me like a son, which meant I was first in line to cop his ill-gotten booty and the title.

I parlayed my degree in mathematics, with a concentration on probability, chance and sporting odds-making, into a career as an insider trader, corporate raider and junk bond dealer before regulation and close scrutiny made that life uncomfortable. Still, Uncle Bertie was so pleased with my success that he put me up for his club.

The Second World War interrupted my career as a City pirate. Following a none-too-subtle hint from my uncle I rashly volunteered for the Royal Navy, naïvely unaware that the chief occupational hazards included drowning, alcohol poisoning, and diseased dockyard doxies. My misplaced fit of patriotism also meant that I was forced to say "Au revoir" to Anastasia for the duration. Before leaving for my first ship, however, as a patriotic gesture I sold the contents of Anastasia's copious petrol tank to a shifty-looking gentleman with a length of rubber hose, a loud check suit, a greasy pork pie hat, and a Clark Gable moustache. Poor Anastasia spent the war years alone, under a dust sheet in my parents' garage.

It was an unhappy separation as I had become very much attached to Anastasia. She was what, in the modern idiom, is called a chick magnet, and one whose passenger seat was rarely unoccupied by a delicate morsel of the opposite sex, all ready, willing, and usually grateful for the ride. When parked, with the hand brake on and the gear lever in neutral, it took only a little imagination for those athletic enough to enjoy the benefits of marriage without the intervention of clergy. For the others, there was always the Savoy or the Dorchester. Only Lady Penelope let the side down a bit, carelessly failing to dodge the fatal bullet, and had to avail herself of the services of her mother's discreet and expensive Harley Street specialist.

When Uncle Bertie cashed in his chips for the last time and was kitted out with his harp and halo, I ended up with the title and what was left of his ill-gotten spoils after the Treasury had plundered the accounts.

Being a Viscount had its advantages (though an earldom has more), especially with a vintage Roller as a prop. Even in later years, after my youthful vigour had begun its inevitable long, shallow glide from chest to waist, the beautiful, the marginal and the downright homely still flocked to my side. It would have been positively churlish for a chap to have disappointed, don't you think?

A British car in those golden days of motoring came with an official document, a folded cardboard log book which I chucked unopened into the glove box. I replaced it with a log book of my own, one which contained the names and addresses of every girl who had ever occupied the seat beside me, and the outcome. This log book tells me that 2,317 women of all ages have graced Anastasia's passenger seat since I turned twenty-one, most of them,

I regret to say, in the first fifty years. Few failed to take advantage of me. I wish I could remember them all.

I keep the log book going still, in case my luck should change, though there have been few entries these past several years. One of the last, I see, was in 1996, when I drove that most gracious and beautiful lady, Sophia Loren to the Cannes Film Festival, and to dinner afterwards where we joined her husband, Carlo Ponti. With the evening spent basking in the golden aura of Ms. Loren, all recollection of her husband escapes me except that, regrettably, he drove her home.

I never married, and it's a bit late to think about it now so the line dies with me. Probably a good thing, all told: I would have made a faithless husband, and it would have meant cheating on Anastasia, my one true mistress. By tacit consent, the aforementioned 2,317 encounters do not count.

I don't get out as much as I used to, and in truth I have hardly driven these past several years. The narrow, steep, and winding streets of Monte Carlo are crowded with Ferraris, Lamborghinis, and Maseratis, the status symbols of the insecure, the upstart nouveau riche and poseurs flaunting their wealth for the benefit of the gawking day-trippers. But with the top down and the wind ruffling what is left of my hair, the Grande Corniche, with its hairpin bends is still an exhilarating drive in Anastasia, even when, as is the case all too often these days, I am alone.

No, I am no longer a downy-cheeked stripling. But we have had a good, long run, Anastasia and I. We have grown old together, she more gracefully than I. I'm not looking forward to my inevitable parting with Anastasia any more than failing my impending interview with St. Peter. However ingenious one may be, it is virtually impossible to cheat on a viva and, I am told, St. Peter does not set a written exam. And so the time has come to pass the torch to a younger man to take my place.

The Spirit of Ecstasy that has adorned Anastasia's bonnet for eighty years is soon bound for another garage and another admirer. It will be necessary, for her sake, to approve the new man in her life. That is not something easily done at an auction. Besides, they're such mercenary affairs, auctions, rarely attracting the right sort of chap, Americans mostly, and that would not do at all. I'd hate to see Anastasia end up in California. She belongs here, in Monte. Or perhaps in London, where she'd be appreciated.

Wherever she spends the rest of her days, I hope she will serve her new man as well and as faithfully as she has served me. I shall put a discreet word around at my club:

"For Sale (With Regret): 1933 Rolls-Royce Phantom II drop-head coupé. Answers to 'Anastasia.' One owner. All original coachwork and equipment. Complete history. Passenger seat may need reupholstering."

Saints and Sinners

Nancy Kay Clark

Who the hell was St. Polycarpe? Heading east from Toronto, the 401 ends when you hit the Quebec border and once you cross the line the town names change from Brockville, Cornwall, and Lancaster to saints. But such strange saints: St. Polycarpe, St. Telesphore, St. Zotique. Never heard of them. What made them saints?

An hour-and-a-half later, we're in St. Eustache, and my father waits for me on the balcony of his third floor condo. He watches as our Toyota pulls into the parking lot. I expected him to be inside and I'm squinting out of the car window, trying to remember what unit number he's in—'cause I've left his address at home on a scrap of paper, neglecting to add it to the contact list on my cell. But he's there waiting for us on the balcony, his white comb-over caught by the summer breeze. He stands, puts up a hand to wave.

We sit on the balcony for a while. We talk about little things. Catch up on family stories. Sort out the parking arrangements for the night. Fuss over whether we should take the umbrella down— the wind is picking up. We laugh over my sister's bossiness, my brother's inability to remember birthdays, my perverse stubbornness in actually living in Toronto. He even asks politely how mum is. His second wife fetches Jeff a beer, me a glass of wine. "Suzanne," my dad calls after her. *"Verre de l'eau s'il te plait."*

"Oui, Coco," she answers.

The next day, Suzanne packs water bottles and snacks for four and we leave in their mini-van. Jeff offers to drive, but my dad has always driven. He tells us about the time he was twenty and had his first job at the bank and one Friday after work he and his brother Robert took his '52 Buick and drove all night to New York City to catch a Rangers game at Madison Square Garden. On Sunday afternoon they raced home, but the Buick broke down just outside Plattsburgh, New York. They had to push it for a mile and a half. They were late for work on Monday.

More stories like this come out of Dad as we take the 15 into Montreal, of him in the '50s, when he was lean and slim and had dark Elvis hair, of when he first met my mom.

After a while Suzanne interrupts to talk about her children. I ask about my half-sister Carole.

"Oh, things aren't going well with Carole," my dad answers, his voice full of outrage. "That ex of hers is really giving her a hard time. He argues about everything. Never pays child-support. How is she supposed to cope? He's a real bastard."

His words hang in the stale air of the van. And then Suzanne switches to their second daughter. "Chantal is doing well. She has a great job with the *caisse populaire*. We like her boyfriend." As always when I speak to my stepmother, she speaks in French; I answer her in English. Neither attempts the other's language, but we understand each other nonetheless.

An hour later we're in the first church Brother—now Saint —Andre built on Mount Royal. The little wooden chapel squats behind the enormous stone St. Joseph's Oratory. We lean on a wooden railing and look through plates of Plexiglas at Brother Andre's bedroom in the 1920s. A life-size mannequin of a four-foot tall stooped old man in black robes stands by a humble desk looking out a small window. Against the opposite wall is his humble single bed.

Visitors have pushed notes through the gaps between the Plexiglas sheets. Mounds of folded multicoloured paper are strewn on the floor behind the glass or stuck half way through the barriers. "They do that," says dad. "People. They ask Brother

Andre to pray for them." Most of the notes are folded tight and you can't read the pleas, but some have fallen open. They are in every language and by different hands, both childish printing and the beautiful penmanship of people born before the computer age: Pray for me, Holy Brother...*Je vous en prie, Mon Seigneur*...I'm sick, my mother's dying, my child is crippled, my dog's been run over, my father has left us. One day he's there, the next he's not. Jeff and I bend down to read the notes through the glass. They are like museum pieces to us—Egyptian hieroglyphs.

My father laughs. "When Suzanne had her aneurism—must be four years ago now—we rushed her to the hospital and I didn't know what would happen. I bought some holy oil from the gift shop here. Brother Andre's holy oil. I kept it by her bedside, put a drop on her forehead." He says this sheepishly—like he can't believe he still believes.

"Well," says Jeff. "Must have worked."

On the way out of the city, my dad drives through Snowdon for me. "Your mother and I had our first apartment in this building. And this, this down here is the church we were married in." He speaks almost fondly of those times. At least it sounds that way to me.

Forty minutes later and we're in Ste. Rose and he drives through the narrow streets and, like we're on a tour bus going through some European town, he starts a running commentary: "This, this big place—oh, it hasn't been kept up—this house on Debuscus we rented when you were a baby. This one here was the curé's house, the church was across the street, on that flat bit. It burned down years ago. This was your grandmother's *depanneur*—they've changed it back into a house. One summer in the back, I opened a *caisse croute*—sold hot dogs and burgers. Called it Dick's Back Snack. I was seventeen. Only lasted a couple of weeks. I got tired of it.

"There's where my brother and I used to play football, there on the field beside the old train station. No more trains now, of course. Oh, I know what I'll show you, when I first met your mother, she was about fifteen maybe, she lived in this tiny house down by the river with Mrs. Cavendish. We used to sit on the porch with our stamp collections, for hours." He drives his large van down this twisty narrow street, close to the river's edge, trying to find a particular house. "I think, I think it was this one." He stops the car beside a tiny nondescript bungalow.

We all look at it in silence. "Mom told me about this place," I say. "It was cold in the winter. They had this one pot-bellied stove, and it flooded every spring." I'm smiling like an idiot.

He does not confirm these facts, but smiles back. Something has been established.

Suzanne coughs.

My father takes me to the graveyard where his mother is buried. It is less impressive than I remember—a chain-fenced block of flat land now surrounded by new duplexes. We all get out of the car. Jeff, amiable and solid, takes my hand. My father leads the way, and when we get there he bends and brushes off dirt from the large stone that marks the graves of eight in the Boulanger/Henderson clan. He cannot stop talking today, and the names on the stone set him off again.

Alphonse Boulanger (1880-1957) *épouse de* Léa Doré (1885-1960). My dad remembers his grandmother Léa as a soft presence sitting by the stove darning socks. He tells me his grandfather Alphonse was half paralyzed from imbibing bad moonshine.

Jean Pierre (1938-1964): "A *petit cousin* of mine," he says. "It was a suicide. We never talked about it, but we all knew."

Albert (1913 to 1968): an uncle who always smoked cigars.

John E. Henderson (1906-1964): Born in Pictou, Nova Scotia, my grandfather on his first trip to the big fleshpot of Montreal met Madeleine—and never went back to Pictou.

Sara (1944-1947): "One day my little sister had a headache," he tells us. "And the next day they took her away. I never saw her again."

Robert J. (1934-1970): My dad's brother, the one who came with him to New York, who played ball with him, his constant boyhood companion, dead at thirty-six from cancer.

And lastly, Madeleine (1909-1984): My gran, who never approved of my father's behaviour.

In the evening, Dad insists on driving north to St. Sauveur for dinner. We sit on the patio of Suzanne's favourite restaurant on the main drag, and watch the fashionable people walk up and down and the motorcycles roar by. My father has his usual: *steak haché et frites* with a Pepsi; Suzanne has Veal Parmesan. Jeff and I share a bottle of wine and contemplate the wilted salads in front of us.

Dad is trying to think of things to say so I ask him something I've always wondered about. "After Uncle Robert died, how come we never saw Tante Sylvie and the cousins much?"

"I couldn't see her. I couldn't." After some prompting, the story spills out of him. "When Robert was dying in the hospital, he called me over and told me he thought his wife was having an affair and asked me to find out for him. I told him he was crazy, but I agreed. So I followed Sylvie one day and she was having an affair. But I went back to Robert and told him she wasn't. He was dying and she was screwing around. I couldn't look her in the face after that. I couldn't forgive her."

I bite my tongue. I'm watching Suzanne, who's looking at her plate, concentrating on cutting her meat. There are some things we never talk about.

That night in the guest bedroom of the condo, Jeff is in a good mood. He knows I've put off this trip to Quebec to visit my dad. "He seems like a good guy to me. He's been very generous with his time, taking us all around. I think he's really trying to do something nice for you."

And I can't entirely disagree.

Arrive at the place you need to be.

"a best and forsaken place"

My Heart's Home

Four Months' Hard Sweeping
Nancy Kay Clark

Sweeping's for old women and crater-faces—everyone knew it wasn't fair! It could have happened to anyone. It wasn't my fault. The judge had it in for me. My mom cried when the judgment came down.

"On the two counts of irresponsibility, how do you find the defendant?"

"Guilty."

"On the count of smugness?"

"Guilty."

"And lastly, on the count of untidiness?"

"Guilty." Then the judge lectured me on how I had endangered the whole community with my sloppy, uncaring attitude; with my inability to keep things in order, blah, blah, blah. The sentence? Four months' hard sweeping. Un-fucking-believable.

"Hey dusthead, wake up!" Someone whacked me on the head in passing. It was my supervisor, No-face Jake. "Get your gear and come on." I gathered up my mask and visor and scrambled after him—waddled after him actually. The orange coveralls I was wearing were gi-normous. Not really a good look for me.

Jake was a veteran sweeper. Rumour had it that he'd been on the job for close to ten years—but that's crap cause nobody lasts ten years sweeping, even with protective gear. Black lung got you long before that. I don't know exactly what happened to his face, but obviously he'd been exposed way back when. One big, bad swoosh of black-green—that was the worst. It ate at flesh like starving rats. Jake's right ear was gone, nibbled down to just a hole, while his right cheek and chin were puckered and cratered. The scar tissue was a dull grey.

I followed Jake into the lunchroom, where a dozen people in orange waited, their masks and visors in their arms. You could tell at a glance the difference between the regulars and the convicts. The regulars were old and crater-faced and hunched over, as if weighed down by piles of dust on their shoulders. They had chosen to be sweepers; had signed up for the job. Whether they'd been scarred before they signed up or got the scars on the job, I didn't know, but all of them carried marks of their encounters with the dust. The other half of the group was young and unmarked and looked terrified; they were my fellow convicts. But I didn't look like that—I didn't—I wasn't scared of anything.

"Okay, listen up, you dustheads!" That's what the regulars called the convicts—don't know why. "I'm going to assign you a senior sweeper for the duration of your stay with us. You are to stick with your sweeper like blue glue. You are to do what your sweeper tells you to do without any lip. You eat when they tell you to, you rest when they tell you to, you shit when they tell you to— that clear, dustheads? I didn't hear you. Is that clear?"

"Yes, Yes sir," we yelled in unison.

"And another thing, today we're staying inside, so it's a bit different. But out in the field, full kit—no exceptions—boots, helmet, gloves, visor, mask. And you never take any of it off. I don't care if it's as still as well water out there—you never take it off. Is that clear? IS THAT CLEAR, DUSTHEADS?"

Jake had a way of thrusting his mangled face into yours when he talked to you—and he really did that now, making sure we all understood what happens when you take off your protective gear. Is that what happened to him? Was he caught without his mask?

I was assigned a sweeper—a regular—named Esmeralda. She was short, tiny, and old with skin like cracked leather. When she smiled at me, her teeth flashed a dull yellow. "Call me Esme," she said and shook my hand like she'd been pumping iron all her life.

"Easy day, easy day today," Esme said. We were assigned to sweep the Maple Grove plaza; it was a Saturday and full of shoppers. Of all the bloody plazas in the entire city, it had to be Maple Grove. That's my plaza. That's the one my friends shop at and their parents and my parents and the friends of my parents. Crap! Esme said I didn't need to keep my mask on in the plaza—it was mostly white dust that got in there and white was harmless—but I kept my mask on anyway.

Esme specialized in detail work. After the main crew passed through with electric vacs, Esme followed, sweeping out the nooks and crannies, cleaning the smaller surfaces, the benches and tables, the counters and screens, every leaf of the plastic maples trees. "Go slow," she said by way of instructions. "Carefully—from left to right, from up to down."

Yeah, whatever. I tried at first, I really did, but it seemed so pointless. I mean you sweep today, and tomorrow you've just got to do it all over again. So my mind wandered. Esme kept scolding me and asking me to do things over. "Too sloppy, be more careful, go slow," she repeated in a constant irritating chorus.

We were in the middle of the grove tackling one of the trees with hand brushes, when I spotted Lisel and Glory talking, strolling right toward me. I ducked behind a tree trunk. Esme chuckled. "Don't worry. They no see you." And she was right—they walked right by me, but never looked at me. How could they not see me?

I was distracted, trying to figure it out. All afternoon I tried to figure it out as other people I knew walked by me without blinking. You'd think they'd notice someone in bright orange.

The next day, Esme and I were sent to recover items from the collapsed section of a nursery school that had been caught in Dust-storm Tina. It had been all over the media—people up in arms accusing the school board of building too close to the surface —the school board blaming the building contractors for faulty construction. Three teachers and twenty-five kids dead. The items had been brought into a clean room set up close to the collapse.

They looked pathetic and a little creepy under their shrouds of dust. It was just Esme and me doing the detail work. We were alone in the room all day long. Esme wouldn't let me take my mask off this time. Full kit, she said, you never knew where a bit of blue glue or black-green could be hovering.

It was my job to immerse the items one by one in a series of vats filled with various cleaning solutions. Some of the cleaning stuff looked disgusting and reeked like vomit. I wanted to get it done and get the hell out of that room, but again Esme insisted otherwise and so I fell into a slow, robotic pace. I had to inspect each item to identify the dust.

Items covered in blue glue were taken up by wooden tongs (never your gloved hands because the blue glue would stick to your gloves) and dumped into a vat of hot fat that dissolved the blue.

Anything with red streaks went into the vinegar vat.

Anything with grey or white went into plain soap and water. Anything with violet splotches went into one of the smelly solutions.

And anything with even a smidgeon of black-green was deemed irretrievable. I packed those in vacuum containers. These items would be removed later and burned as fuel in the city furnaces. Once the items had soaked in their various vats, Esme would take each out, rinse them in clean water and wipe them off with a soft cloth.

I was soon bored and sleepy. I kept yawning under my mask. I can't tell you how much time went by. It could have been ten minutes or three hours. I don't know. Then I heard humming. It took me a while to figure it out; it was coming from Esme. She hummed and muttered ever so slightly as she worked. She'd pick an item out of the vat with her strainer and then talk to it—like she was talking to a baby.

She scooped up a dollhouse table and its four miniature chairs, and crooned to them: "There, there, it's all right now my little chicks." She dropped them gently in the rinse vat and asked them: "Doesn't that feel nice" And then she picked them out, one by one, from the water and meticulously dried every inch of them. Her soft cloth caressed the beat-up plastic as if it were something rare and fragile. And then she placed the furniture on the clean tray —the table in the middle, the four chairs tucked in around it, just waiting for the dolls to come in and set the table, or for the dead children to come back and play.

*

In the evenings we had to endure group sessions. Monday's lecture was about the importance of civil obedience, of the communal commitment and vigilance against ever-encroaching dust and decay. Tuesday evening we all slept through the procedures of maintaining a dust-free zone. It was kindergarten stuff. Wednesday's session was entitled, "Dust and your Health" and the gruesome images and medical horror stories were a big hit with my fellow convicts. Thursday was "National Sweeper Day" and they told us in nauseating detail about Mrs. Elba Maroni who swept the children's park in Little Etna every day—morning, noon, and night —for thirty years, thus keeping the black lung stats in Little Etna's children under five per cent They gave her a medal—a month before she died of COPD. I'd heard these types of sweeper-hero stories all my life—so barely listened. It was bullshit—no one really important or really smart ever became a sweeper. Friday night was marginally better. We went through safety drills to prepare us for emergencies in the field: what to do if you get blue glue in your eyes or black-green on your skin. "Kiss your face good-bye," murmured the guy beside me. But in fact there was stuff you could do—and I found myself listening.

I was looking forward to the Saturday social—until someone told me that "social" was code for confessional. Basically all us convicts had to get up, one by one, and confess our crimes in front of the group. At first, being curious about my fellow convicts, I thought that might be interesting. Then, I realized I'd have to stand and 'fess up myself and I started to freak out. In the lunchroom on Saturday, Esme sat down across from me and asked me what was the matter.

"Nothing," I said, shrugging.

"Nothing," she said in that soft voice of hers. "Nothing at all?" And when I didn't answer and we had sat in silence for a while, Esme started to tell me this story—it was the most she had ever said to me in one go. She said: "One day, when I was twelve, my mother went to the store and left me with my baby brother. But I didn't want to look after him; I wanted to be with my friends. So I took him to the playground and put him in a baby swing, swung him a few times, left him there and then went over to my friends at the monkey bars. He was only a few feet away; I could see him, keep an eye on him. I thought he was safe. Then my friend Zellie said something to me and I turned to answer her and I heard this swoosh behind me, I turned back and the ceiling had collapsed on top of the swings and all this dust had come pouring in. There was just this mound of dust where the swings had been. Before anyone could stop me I was digging in the dust with my bare hands looking for my brother—that's how I got these." She spread her scarred hands out on the table. "It was stupid. My brother was already dead, of course. That's my confession."

"Your confession?" I said in confusion. "Your confession?"

She nodded her head. "So you won't feel too bad confessing your crime."

How did she know what was bothering me? Never mind that, why did she think her confession would help? "It's not the same!" I said, trying to keep my voice low, so no one else would hear.

"It is the same. I was neglectful—I killed someone."

"It's not the same!" I said, now irritated. "Esme, you were never convicted of disorder were you?"

"No, but still..."

"You didn't know the ceiling was going to collapse. You weren't to blame."

"I was to blame. I failed to keep him safe."

"Oh God, Esme. Is anybody ever safe in this dump?" I said with all the sweeping wisdom of my sixteen years.

But on this point Esme was adamant. "People can be safe, if we sweep carefully, slowly, thoughtfully every day."

I began to laugh at Esme's joke, sweeping thoughtfully, good one, but then I realized that Esme was serious—and possibly certifiable.

"Is that why you became a regular sweeper Esme, because your brother died?"

She nodded her head.

"I never killed anyone, you know," I said to her. "It wasn't like that."

"I know," she said, patting my hand with one of her rough, scarred ones. "But you could have."

*

That evening I stood up in front of everyone and confessed my crime. For all my anxiety beforehand, it was really a non-event. I said it in one go: I was on mandatory community watch one night —all high schoolers have to do it—and I took off early with Glory and forgot to shut the door to the dust collectors. A couple of cats got into them, tracked the dust everywhere. Stuff was ruined, people were scared and the community had to pay overtime for clean up.

"That's it? You killed a couple of cats?" yelled someone from the audience.

"No, the cats were fine. It was grey," I yelled back.

"Shit, you got a crap judge."

I grinned; at last someone agreed with me—that I shouldn't have received such a harsh sentence. But then, No-face Jake dismissed me with a curt cliché: "A place for everything and everything in its place—that keeps us safe" and from the audience I could see Esme nod in agreement with him.

Two weeks, three weeks, one month, and then another month went by—always the same, always doing detail work, in the plazas and offices, in the parks and playgrounds.

New evening programs were invented to bore us or gross us out. At first I slept walked through everything, didn't care anymore that nobody recognized me in the plazas. But gradually I began to notice things—little things. How whenever a civilian stared at Jake's

147

scars he thrust his ravaged chin out even more, and barked his orders even louder. That made me smile. I saw how sloppy and oblivious the civilians were—littering, dropping crumbs everywhere, tracking in the dust, and never closing the bulkheads properly. I had been like that once, I suppose. But mostly I noticed Esme. She never rushed—never. Her hands were so still. Every time I saw the scars, I pictured her frantically digging in the dust to find her baby brother. It was weird to think of her as frantic. And always she hummed. When she was particularly pleased, when I had managed to clean an item slowly and carefully enough, her humming would grow more melodious. When displeased, her humming was a lament, full of keening and low tsks and huffs. I found myself longing for her soft melodies and working hard to earn them.

You're going to think I'm crazy, but there's satisfaction in an item well swept and a place put to rights. One day, I was given the job of sweeping out a courtyard with a manual broom—somehow they couldn't get the electric vacs in there. It was a long and tedious process, and I fully expected to be bored, but I wasn't. Instead with each sweep, I imagined all the dangers in the world, all the chaos, and shitty things that happen to you, being pushed out. I imagined myself marking the boundaries, declaring to I don't know who—to God, I suppose, or the devil or randomness—you cannot step over these lines, as long as I sweep, as long as I sweep, you have to stay out. And I believed that.

The next day, we were sent back to that collapsed nursery school. The city engineers had given us the okay as far as structural repairs were concerned. They had patched the ceiling and hoisted heavy scaffolding all around to guard against the shifting, creeping dust in the crawl spaces between the ceiling and the floor above. The heavy-duty vacs had come in and cleaned out most of the rooms. It was ready for the detail work. We went in with full kit. We had our first aid bag, our water. We were always cautious—safety first with Esme, all the time. She was in a good mood. She was cleaning the counters while I swept the chairs—slowly, carefully, left to right, up to down, just as she had taught me. Esme began one of her happy hums and I was happy too.

I had my back to her when I heard the swoosh. I turned around and Esme was gone. All I saw was black-green. And I remembered the safety procedures from the Friday evening programs—grey and white pour water; red streaks pour vinegar, blue-glue wrap in oily bandages, purple splotches plaster on that smelly shit, but black-green, black-green, you had two, three minutes tops to get it off before the victim became irretrievable—I dug in the dust frantically through the black-green, but there was so much of it. Too much. I couldn't find her.

And that's how I got these scars. I'd had my safety gloves on, but it ate through them and into my hands because I kept on digging long after I should have stopped. It was useless, of course. After five minutes, even with her full kit on, she was gone. The rest of my sentence was waived and I spent a year in a rehabilitation centre for the scarred—waiting for my hands to heal. Two days after I left the hospital, I went to see Jake and signed up as a regular. Anyway, that's my confession—that's why I became a sweeper.

The Final Curtain

Phyllis Humby

They joined hands, one upon the other, in the centre of the table.

One of the five women beamed a triumphant smile. Another had tears sliding across her lined cheeks. With their collective age being just a pinch shy of 400 years, they each realized the gravity of their decision.

Sonya pulled away from the group and headed for the kitchen, for it was in Sonya's home they were gathered. She paused in the hallway that led from the dining room. Framed black and white photographs of her sculptured body lined the wall. Shadow boxes displayed pointes, slippers, and tiaras. There was even a porcelain medallion of her likeness. After all these years, her face flushed with recollections of being a Prima Ballerina.

A burst of laughter—possibly Rosylin's—spurred her on towards the kitchen. Her custom-made ebony cane thumped along the hardwood, then onto the ceramic tiles. Sonya's lips pursed at the sight of the teapot and butter tarts on the tray. Too mundane to memorialize this evening's pledge.

Working swiftly, she topped crackers with goat cheese, slivers of lemon, and smoked oysters. After a sprinkle of fresh chives, she gave a satisfied nod. From the wine fridge, she retrieved a bottle she had been saving for...well, she'd never had an occasion in mind when she'd brought it back from France.

"Could someone please give me a hand," she called out.

Daphne and Clarissa's chatter preceded them to the kitchen. Then Daphne, pear-shaped with hair an unusual shade of orange, and wearing her ever-present over-sized glasses, entered the room with the willowy Clarissa at her side.

"Good," Sonya said, "You two can bring glasses and the Nicolas Feuillatte. Pop the cork in here in case it makes a mess."

Clarissa opened the cabinet and hesitated. "Sonya, could we use these glasses tonight? I've always preferred them to flutes."

Sonya lifted one of the old-style champagne saucers from the shelf and turned it in her hand. Her expression grew melancholy. "We drank our share of champagne over the years," she said then turned to her friend and laughed. "And we certainly didn't drink it from a fluted glass."

Leaning heavily on her cane, Sonya carried the hors d'oeuvres to the dining room. The women cheered as Daphne filled their glasses.

Toasts echoed across the table: "To Friendship…To Memories…To All the Men We've Loved…" With that last toast, began a lively and uncensored exchange of courtships, illicit affairs, and backstage romances. It seemed that no secrets would go to the grave.

Sonya mused that she and her friends had not been this animated and happy in…well, she couldn't recall. They were all in dire circumstances. But whether in ill health or financial ruin, they had something in common—passion. And each had the honour of being extolled as one of the best in her profession.

But that was long ago. Memories were fading. Especially for Judith. Of course, she still had her good days—like today—but increasingly they passed in a fog. Most times, she didn't recognize the auburn-haired siren with pouty red lips and shapely legs in the picture in her room at Greenhaven.

Poor Judith, once the most celebrated pinup in the world, now sipped her glass of champagne with her ever-present doll perched on her lap. Judith had no children, though there were rumours.

Sonya knew the combination of oysters and champagne had never agreed with Clarissa, but her friend ate and drank without reserve. Really, at this point, what difference did it make?

"I can't find my pad and pen," Daphne said.

It didn't come as a surprise. She was searching through Rosylin's tote bag instead of her own. "No more champagne for you," they teased.

Daphne liked to record snippets of conversation. Not that any of the women were concerned about indiscretions being revealed. No one would be reading Daphne's notes. Not because they were indecipherable—which they were—but because no one was interested in anything Daphne wrote. Had not been for years. It was heartbreaking, really. Her first novel had won a Pulitzer Prize. That was sixty years ago. Three of her novels had become award-winning movies. All in the distant past.

Daphne lived with a nephew and his family who, in her own words, had "sucked her dry" years earlier. She now resided in their attached garage.

The champagne had raised the volume of voices, and now Clarissa and Rosylin swayed with arms linked, as they sang "This Old Gal of Mine." Sonya smiled. Sweet, sweet girls—Rosylin and Clarissa. Distant cousins, they'd always claimed. More like kissing cousins. As close as all of the women were, Rosylin and Clarissa remained discreet about their relationship.

When the last appetizer was swallowed and the champagne finished, Sonya addressed her friends. "It's late. We've all been drinking. I think you should stay here for the night."

Everyone spoke at once. Though they'd all shared just one bottle of bubbly, at their age it was more than enough to make them giddy. A short phone call was made to Judith's caretakers, explaining that she was enjoying her old movies and would spend the night. Daphne wouldn't be missed. Her nephew and his family were away. Rosylin and Clarissa, each with terminal cancer, lived together, as they had since their mid-thirties when Rosylin was at the peak of her singing career. They notified their housekeeper that they wouldn't be coming home.

Sonya straightened her aching leg and studied her dear friends. All with wrinkles, swollen ankles, thinning hair, and other less obvious issues. Each of them suffering, either emotionally or physically. Dignity was sliding from their grasp. Life was bad and they all acknowledged it was only going to get worse. Worse. A sobering thought.

With the help of her cane, Sonya inched to her feet and limped to the kitchen. She needed quiet to think. She rubbed her leg, absently easing off her shoes. Though the pain was increasing each day, she still refused to use the wheelchair that gathered dust in her room. She tugged at her support stockings until she was able to remove them. Her tortured feet and twisted toes felt clammy against the tiled floor. Though difficult to walk in bare feet, Sonya carried a second bottle of champagne to her guests. "Come, we'll be more comfortable in the sitting room."

Once they'd settled, Sonya again depended on Daphne to open the wine.

"In this room?" Daphne said. "What about..."

"Don't worry," Sonya told her. "Let the cork fly."

Foam spewed onto the Chippendale table. Gasps and giggles. Everyone held out her glass. After the first sip, Sonya called for their attention. All eyes met hers.

"We've talked about it for months. Tonight we committed ourselves. If you're sure of your decision, and have no qualms or reservations, why should we plan to do it in a week or two? We're the happiest and most carefree tonight as we've been in years."

Rosylin spoke first. "Do you mean we should do it tonight? Now?"

Clarissa clutched Rosylin's hand. When they looked at each other, Sonya detected an imperceptible nod.

Daphne tossed down her pen. "Yes. I say, yes."

"Judith?" Sonya leaned forward. "Judith, do you understand?"

Tears squeezed through her closed lids as she pressed her doll against her shoulder. The faded beauty nodded.

"We need to hear you say it, Judith."

"I'm ready to die."

Sonya's breath caught in her throat. "Bring your glasses of champagne and come with me."

Her four friends followed her to the other room and watched as she opened a drawer in the hutch. She reached beneath a stack of linen napkins for a zip lock bag containing the powdery substance.

Lifting a spoon from the silverware case, she said, "Put a rounded spoonful in your glass. You'll feel drowsy…at first…then nothing."

In silence, they each followed her instruction, then shuffled back to the sitting room. Sonya dumped her spoonful back in the baggie.

When she entered the room, her friends looked calm and composed. There was no hysteria. Their expressions could be described as determined and prepared. They all raised their glasses in a toast: "To the glorious life we knew." They drank, and without hesitation, all of the women swished the last dregs in their glasses and finished their deadly cocktails.

Rosylin put her arms around Clarissa. "Clari, I'm so happy you and I will leave together. Our love will last for all eternity."

Clarissa's wet, time-worn eyes passed from each woman to the next. "We're not cousins. You know that, right?"

"We know," Daphne said, laughing. "Everyone knows how much you love each other."

"Over fifty years now." Clarissa wiped a tear from Rosylin's cheek.

They snuggled into each other and closed their eyes.

Judith curled her long legs under her and rested her head on the arm of the love seat. She kissed her dolly and cuddled down as if preparing for a night's sleep.

Daphne grasped Sonya's hand. "This is the right thing to do. We cannot live the way we want, but at least we can die the way we want." She motioned to her friends in the softly lit room. "Here in the circle of friendship. Not in a makeshift garage." Her chin quivered with those last words.

Tired and emotionally drained, Sonya closed her eyes and focused on the laboured breathing of her precious friends. She had felt a responsibility to see them into the twilight before she went herself.

When she detected no sound, Sonya rose from her seat. The soft glow of the lamps shone on the forms of the elderly women. Only Judith remained breathing. Puffs of air barely parted her lips. It would be over soon.

And what would become of them now, she wondered? Who would bury them? And where? Sonya groaned aloud. She hadn't thought this part through. Her work was not yet finished.

She plodded back through the hallway, pausing again at the framed photos and shadow boxes. The force of her cane shattered the glass. She yanked a sparkling tiara from the velvet background and tucked the bruised slippers under her arm.

Frightened of having a heart attack, she stopped to rest, only continuing when her breathing was normal. She couldn't let her friends down now. With great effort, she moved to the kitchen.

She lowered herself into the chair where her stockings lay in a heap. The tiara tottered on her head as she tried to force her crippled feet into the satin forms. With a sob, she flung the slippers and the tiara across the room, glad that she hadn't humiliated herself in front of the others.

Sonya gathered an armload of newspapers from the recycle bin and hobbled back to the living room. She leaned over her dear friend Judith. No trace of life. She'd joined the others.

Unwavering, Sonya wept as she crumpled the newspapers and placed them around the room and beneath the furniture. She was certain the others would approve. It was better than lying under a sheet with a toe tag, waiting for someone—anyone—to claim you.

Sonya emptied the remaining powder in her glass and tipped more champagne from the bottle. After a brief pause to catch her breath and allow the fast acting potion to begin its work, she reached for the matches.

Wilma

Michael Joll

Wilma watched helplessly as the long, thin tendrils drifted westward towards her on the slight breeze. The vines met, entwining and forming a pale green mat of ground-hugging chlorine gas. Blindness and death slipped snake-silent into the trench she shared unseen with crouching, cowering, praying, suffocating men. The gas insinuated her nose, clutched her throat, seared the moist tissue and infused her lungs, its grip seeking to snuff the life from her like it had Carl's great uncle, Private Joseph Redekopp, at Ypres a hundred years ago.

Joseph's creased face in the sepia photograph on the mantelpiece above the fireplace in her bedroom vanished as Wilma awoke, gasping for air in the still of a humid early August night. The rank sweat of fear mingling with heat sweat seeped into her cotton nightdress. Panic. Asthma attack. She could scarcely breathe with the elephant crushing her chest. She reached for her puffer on her nightstand and inhaled, holding her breath until she believed her lungs would burst. She exhaled, took a second puff, holding it in until the invisible corset binding her torso began to release its stranglehold. Her panic slowly subsided, dissolving as the asthma medication did its work. She would not suffocate, not this time.

She heard thunder rumble in the distance, over Goderich way, she reckoned. Maybe closer. Listowel. It will be here soon, she

156

told herself and hoped it would not damage the cereal crops. She opened her eyes, staring at the bedroom ceiling. A tiny breath of air swayed the sheers covering her open window, barely movement enough to catch her eye in the darkness. The wind gusted and the sheers billowed. Moonlight and sheet lightning flickered off her dressing table mirror, casting distorted shadows across the floral wallpaper.

Wilma closed her eyes, willing herself to relax, letting the asthma medication do its work, but she held her puffer tightly in her grasp in case she needed a third dose. She kicked the sheets down around her ankles, letting the light breeze cool her slight body while she listened to the sounds of the gathering storm.

"Carl," she whispered as her hand reached out across the empty half of their bed, the only bed that either had ever shared, now too big for one person. More than anything she needed her husband to assure her that all was well, but the sheet was cool to her touch. Carl was no longer there. Dear Carl. Her husband for more than forty-five years no longer lay beside her. It had been that way for almost six years, ever since the accident that she was sure was no accident, no matter what the others said, had claimed his life.

All the Redekopps had raised barns since they were barely old enough to walk, without ever so much as a misstep. To reshingle the roof of the farmhouse was an elementary task hardly worthy of Carl's skill, but it needed to be done. As she left for the Co-Op in St. Jacob's that afternoon, she called out of the truck window, "Be sure you're careful, Carl." He waved back from the foot of the ladder with a bundle of shingles over his shoulder and said something that she could not quite hear as she accelerated away towards the road.

Returning from her trip a couple of hours later she found the chickens out of their coop, milling about on the driveway. She drove carefully through them, scattering the squawking grey-brown clouds. She found Carl's body alongside the fallen ladder on the patch of grass in front of their living room window. A bundle of shingles lay scattered on the ground beside him with their boar snorting contentedly and rooting about Carl's lifeless body.

Wilma screamed. The boar looked up, eyed her, grunted, and then turned its attention back to Carl's flesh. Wilma ran up the steps, pushed open the front door and tripped over the body of their lifeless lab-collie mix sprawled on the floor with its side ripped open. She screamed again, turned her head to block out the sight and stumbled across the living room. In Carl's desk drawer she found the key to the gun cabinet, unlocked the cabinet next to the fireplace and with trembling hands loaded the twelve gauge with two shells from the box in Carl's desk.

She stepped outside with ice in her heart, took aim and squeezed both triggers. The recoil flung her onto her back but the boar lay dead. Dazed, she glanced up and saw the gate to the pig's sty swinging on its hinges. They never left the gate open. The boar never left his sty; they brought the sows to him. Moreover, the chickens never left their enclosure except to make an appearance at the table for Sunday dinner.

Wilma voiced her suspicions to the police officer and again at the inquest, but the coroner returned a finding of accidental death. At Carl's funeral, her friends and neighbours gathered around her and comforted her, pledging their support, but her heart kept asking, "Which one of you killed him? Why?"

Wilma kept her thoughts about the strange circumstances of her husband's death to herself. She carried on working the farm with help from the sons of her nearest neighbour, Carl's cousin Rudi. Although it cut into her savings and the farm income, she paid them for their work and with cheerful good humour they took on the backbreaking tasks she could no longer manage. But costly machinery repairs that Carl used to do himself she now had to pay for. A grass fire destroyed the drive shed. When the tractor mysteriously would not start right before ploughing time she had to leave fallow twenty prime acres that she could not reach before heavy autumn rains made ploughing impossible. The year after Carl died, for the first time the farm operated at a loss, and she was ashamed when word got out.

Rudi offered to buy the farm, but Wilma refused to sell. "You know Carl inherited the farm," she told him. "It's the best acreage for miles around, and I'll work it until the day I join him in the churchyard. Everyone knows we've no children, and just about everyone knows the church and its charities are the sole beneficiaries of my will. The church will auction off the farm when my time comes. You can buy it then." It was what she and Carl had decided, decades before and she wasn't about to change her mind or her will. "And," she warned Rudi darkly, "Heed the tenth commandment: Thou shalt not covet." Rudi had brought the matter up a couple of times since, the last time right after the tractor broke down, but her answer was the same: Thou shalt not covet.

Her doubts about Carl's death remained. "All these little things that keep going wrong, they can't all be bad luck, can they?" she asked Rudi during a break at the Christmas euchre tournament.

"No such thing as luck," he told her as they took their places back at the card table. "It's God's will, a test of faith."

"It's more than a run of bad luck," she muttered as Rudi turned his attention to his cards. "God's will be damned!" Wilma fanned her cards and covered her mouth, consumed with guilt at her blasphemy.

The memories melted in the warm night until she no longer recognized them. A breeze drifted through the sheers into her bedroom, cooling her hot body. She closed her eyes. Drowsy again, sleep coming. The gas had not killed her, not like Joseph, not this time. "Thank you, Lord for sparing my life once more," she whispered. Silently, she began to recite the Lord's Prayer.

A noise broke through her drowsiness; a noise so faint that she could not identify it, but definitely one that did not belong in the farmhouse. Nor outside. Inside, she was sure, downstairs, a piece of furniture moving, perhaps a chair scraping across the pine floor of the living room. She held her breath, alert, her eyes wide open as fear preyed on her imagination, listening, hoping, and praying that it was nothing.

She checked the clock on the night stand: 4:18 a.m.—too early for Rudi's sons to start the daily chores, and they never came into the house anyway unless she invited them in for a glass of lemonade or a can of pop.

She heard the noise again. Was it a faint footfall, a scuff, something being moved a fraction of an inch? Could it be the bones of the house? No, she was sure it wasn't the bones. It has to be someone making the noise, an intruder.

The smell of fear flooded her armpits again, invading her nostrils as she craned her head to see who might at any second enter her bedroom.

Silence…then thunder, close this time, masking the soft scuffing. The rumble died away. A creak…the stairs? A mouse? There are plenty of mice around the farm. "No, it has to be someone," she heard herself whisper, though it brought no comfort. Choking stomach acid lurched into her throat. "Don't panic. Don't cough. Breathe naturally."

She reached slowly for the phone beside the clock, picked the handset carefully from the cradle and put it to her ear. No dial tone. She pressed the cradle softly, twice. Nothing but unbroken silence…

Another creak. It had to be the second step from the bottom of the flight leading to her bedroom, the one that always creaked underfoot. Thunder rumbled overhead as the phone slipped from her fingers onto the bedside mat. The phone's muffled thud startled her. Fear renewed its grip on her chest, squeezing and paralyzing her body.

The asthma returned. She couldn't breathe but didn't dare take a third puff. Whoever was in the house might see her move and know she was awake. She gripped her inhaler and slipped her hand under her body where her murderer would not see it. She screwed her eyelids tight. Blind panic and her asthma forced her mouth open. She took a breath and tried to scream but no sound came.

The constriction in her chest would not let her exhale. The nightmare pale green tendrils of chlorine gas had found her lungs. This, she knew with absolute certainty, was her time to die, alone and terrified, at one with Carl and poor Joseph in his trench, flailing, twitching, and then still. She wet herself, the warm and comforting fluid soaking through her nightdress into her mattress.

Her bedroom door cracked open. She lay rigid, feigning sleep, praying that whoever it was would leave without killing her. "Please God," she begged silently. "Make him go away before he smells my fear and knows I'm awake. Please... Please...

"Dear God, let me live to die in peace, not murdered like my Carl."

Thunder crashed directly overhead. A fork of lightning lit the bedroom with intense, stark white light, forcing her eyes open for a split second, but she could not make out for certain the face of the man looming over her. She thought she caught a glimpse of red under the ball cap. A hint, no more. Rudi had red hair. So did his sons. All the Redekopps had red hair, she knew, as far back as Uncle Joseph's time and probably beyond. Carl had called red hair the family curse, but in the utter blackness that followed the blinding flash she could not absolutely swear on the bible that the hair was red.

The intruder turned and tiptoed away. The second to bottom tread of the stairs creaked. Did he see my eyes open, she wondered? When she heard a muffled curse as the intruder bumped into Carl's old Lazy-Boy, she knew he hadn't. Above the storm she heard a different, unnatural sound—the front door closing with a click. He was gone. "Thank you, Lord, for sparing my life," she mouthed. She grabbed her inhaler and sucked on it.

The wind picked up, catching the screen door, banging it hard against the frame, again and again as the thunderstorm crashed about her, hurling sheets of rain across the fields of wheat and barley, flattening the ripening harvest in its fury.

The elephant eased its weight off her chest. She breathed more easily, then screamed, a long, ululating wail carried away on the wind. She slid from her bed and crawled to the bedroom door.

*

When the brothers found the truck parked in the driveway but no sign of Wilma they went home and told their father. Rudi found Wilma that afternoon squatting in her foul, sodden nightdress with her eyes screwed shut, slowly rocking back and forth beneath a row of frocks hanging neatly from the rack above her in her closet, whimpering. In her hands she clutched Carl's loaded shotgun.

Wilma never left the psychiatric hospital. Rudi's sons bought the farm when the church sold it at auction, "To keep it in the family," they explained. "It's what our father would have wanted." Folk around St. Jacob's nodded their approval and figured they paid a fair price for it—considering.

My Heart's Home
Phyllis Humby

The End

Though the nights were still punishing, with every day that passed, an oppressive weight lifted and my mood lightened.

While touring the Irish Loop these past few weeks, I'd travelled this very road and sat on the rocks at the beach in Chapel's Cove—salt water on my lips, the sun on my face, and the sound of lilting dialect drifting through open windows. Thus began my love affair with Newfoundland.

More interested in the scenery than the realtor's running monologue, I twisted in my seat for a better view of the familiar landmarks. The rhythm of the windshield wipers and the whir of the tires against the wet asphalt lulled me into a composed but expectant frame of mind. Absorbed in every feature of the undisturbed country setting, I became more excited as we drew closer to our destination.

Ryan Howard prattled non-stop as we followed the curving roadway along the irregular shoreline to Chapel's Cove from his office in Bay Roberts.

"Yessir, born and raised right 'ere. Never give a thought to leavin'. Nosir. Lucky to be in the real estate. Always somethin' happening, right?" Mr. Howard turned to me as if making sure I was listening and then continued, "Yessir, them trades boys ended up way the hell and gone to Fort McMurray, the most of them. 'Spose some settled in Ontario."

His voice droned on in a steady litany while my mind whirled in reflection.

My husband—ex-husband—was never far from my thoughts. We had planned for years to take a family vacation to Newfoundland, but the time was never right. The brochures featuring the rugged coastline and colourful fishing shanties had me dreaming of whale watching with the grandchildren, feasting on fresh lobster, and snapping pictures of puffins. My dream holiday never materialized. Frankly, our vacations never turned out as planned. There was always bickering, tension, and hurt feelings —mostly mine.

This part of the country, two thousand miles from home, seemed like the perfect escape. Although concerned for my welfare and state of mind, my son and daughter didn't interfere when I booked my getaway. Now, God help me, I was planning more than a vacation.

Travelling the shoreline of the saltwater bay along the familiar Route 60, I was convinced now, more than ever, that this real estate listing on Old Broad Road was my salvation. Old Broad Road, indeed.

Mr. Howard's vehicle lurched over the mud-packed ruts, and my hand gripped the door handle. We slowed to a stop, the ocean barely visible beyond the densely treed lot. Before he had turned off the ignition, the muddy driveway was tugging at the soles of my shoes.

"Let's check the property first," I said, without a sideways glance at the empty house.

The smell of wet vegetation and seawater created a nervous flutter, like butterflies batting against my ribcage. Despite my mounting apprehension, I felt an urgent need to explore. Not waiting for the agent, I hurried to the back of the yard. Seeing the salt-water bay and the jagged rocks calmed me in spite of the exhilaration I felt.

The agent's voice interrupted my thoughts. "Miz Kramer? You're not dressed for this damp marnin'. Let's go inside, now."

My stomach heaved with nerves. The fear of being sick in front of this stranger was a growing worry, but there was no turning back. Chapel's Cove would be my retreat. My refuge. Despite the anticipated backlash of Dan and Darlene, I wasn't going back to Toronto.

"Yes, this is it. I'm sure." I nodded toward the view.

His eyes widened and he stepped towards me.

"You haven't seen the inside of the house, maid. 'Tis fairly isolated here and I don't think you know what our winters are like." His strong east-coast accent made him difficult to understand. "You'd be lonely as a gull on a rock living 'ere." His considerable weight shifted from one foot to the other, his face wrinkling into a whine.

"If I didn't know better I'd say you didn't want to make a sale this morning." My voice inflected a haughty tone—one I had perfected over the years.

Turning toward the abandoned house, I glanced down at my sodden canvas shoes feeling the wetness soak through to my socks. The rain had stopped and I closed my eyes and inhaled. The smell of the damp earth aroused a childhood memory of shiny worms inching across a wet sidewalk. Recollections of my life before I became a wife and mother—a grandmother—were rare.

A cool wet breeze dampened my hair, its mist settling into the deep lines around my eyes. I turned back to the magnificent view. During the weeks spent touring Canada's east coast, I dreamed of living here, though never expected anything to come of it. Pretending was part of my healing process. Pretending to be alone in the world gave me solace. Feeling the undeniable need to be alone on the beach at night. To scream at the top of my lungs into the crashing waves. Nighttime was when I ranted and cried. That's when I felt old and unhinged.

The agent ended my wandering thoughts with an attention-getting grunt and a dubious look.

"I do plan on checking the house, Mr. Howard." I could hear that my jangled nerves added a harsh edge to my tone. I turned from the crest of the craggy coastline and looked up at the weathered frame edifice. Clinging to the back of the house was a wooden deck atop supports from the sloped landscape. Its stilt-like structure appeared to tremble with the strong breeze.

Water-drenched weeds tangled around my ankles like restraints to keep me from entering the house, which at a glance looked old and unloved—much like the way I felt. The realtor appeared relieved when I moved towards the dwelling. Seeing the decaying bottom step of the raised deck, I changed direction and led the way to the front door.

Mr. Howard followed so closely behind me that I could hear his ragged breathing and smell the lingering smoke on his clothes. As a reformed smoker, the smell was neither tempting nor revolting, but something my nose immediately identified.

Through the open screen door, the inside entry room looked battered, with peeling paint and a general tired appearance. I was beginning to understand the realtor's skepticism.

The house key worked, but not without difficulty.

"This won't be too good, I imagine, now maid. The good Lord only knows what we'll be finding inside." He stepped aside and allowed me to enter the enclosed sun porch.

My heart was thumping with the realization of what I was doing and the finality of it. On my own for the first time and trembling with fright, I did not want anyone to think I was incompetent, least of all this agent. I'd smile until my face hurt if that would make me appear at ease and in control.

Two mice skittered across the room when the screen door banged behind us. I smiled and stepped over the splintered threshold of the screened porch. It would take more than mice to deter me.

The house was in a dilapidated state with faded wallpaper, pockmarked woodwork, and yellowed ceiling tiles. We turned down the hallway to our right and poked our heads into a small bathroom. Linoleum tiles curled around the base of a dingy toilet, the wooden seat and lid scarred and slightly askew.

The chipped enamel sink had a single tap and an empty chain hanging from the spout. Rust trailed to the drain like dried blood from an open wound. A curtain drooped over the opening of the small shower. I nudged it aside. Long-legged spiders danced around the webbed drain of the mildew-stained enclosure.

The tongue and groove bottom portion of the wall needed painting and hideous brown and yellow wallpaper partially covered the top half of the room.

"You must be saving the best for last, Mr. Howard." My chuckle ended in a choked cough.

"I don't believe there is a best in this forsaken place. We can leave whenever you like, now."

There was a small room with peeling wallpaper at the end of the hallway. It may have been a bedroom, although there were no built-in closets or cupboards. It was unnerving the way the realtor kept looking at me, as if watching for a look of disapproval, but I did my best not to show emotion. I had already determined this would be my home.

A few shallow breaths enabled me to retreat up the hall past the threshold of the sun porch. A narrow room stretched toward a large window with smaller, sliding panes with screens. The warped paneling on the walls created a wavy effect.

Soot from the wood stove speckled the ash-scarred floor, while the sickening smell of creosote and disuse tormented my nostrils. At this point, a bulldozer seemed like the best idea. Then I entered the next room.

Walking past the stairs in the living room, the doorway off to the right revealed the kitchen. Something about the large square room captured my imagination. Not even the diaper in the garbage pail affected my enthusiasm. Nor did the prevalent smell of grease, or the dangling wire in the centre of the ceiling with a single bulb attached.

Mr. Howard didn't follow me into the room but watched from the doorway while I scanned the dreary space. My unexpected excitement overshadowed the encrusted dirt on the floor that outlined the area that the refrigerator had once occupied, and the four-burner stove littered with mice offerings that was jammed between the plywood cupboards. It was crazy, but the potential for this kitchen thrilled me.

"I'm sure you didn't expect anything this bad." His sidelong glance told me he thought I might bolt at any moment.

I shrugged and headed for the narrow stairs situated along the wall separating the living room from the kitchen. My damp rubber soles squeaked across the wooden floor until I was standing at the bottom of a narrow enclosed staircase. I reached for the two-by-four handrail and took my time climbing the steep ascent until the dust covered plank floor came into view. A few more steps. The airless atmosphere sucked the breath out of me. A hallway led to four tiny bedrooms and an unfinished framed-in storage area. Dirty windows allowed little light to enter. There was nothing to see—not even closets, but already an idea tugged the corner of my mouth into a wannabe grin.

Cautious on the shallow steps, I turned partially sideways to descend to the main floor.

I wandered back through the living room and into the kitchen, pausing to peer through the discoloured lace curtain on the rear door. It was lucky that I hadn't chanced walking on the deteriorating surface of the deck. With my gaze fixed on the rotted boards, my mind flashed back to an elaborately furnished patio, brick barbeque, and manicured lawn. I closed my eyes, shutting out the memory.

Back in the living room, the unwashed window allowed a filtered view of the cliffside that caught my breath moments earlier —copse of trees, rugged round boulders, jagged rocks. The ocean. I could hear it now. Or could I? I caught a glimpse of a pathway leading down the embankment. Ryan Howard interrupted my musings. His restless hands toyed with the loose change in his pockets, suggesting a growing impatience. Perhaps he needed a smoke. His tuneless whistling was annoying.

"Sorry to hold you up. It's a lot to take in all at once. I may be moving slowly but a decision like this..." I swallowed past the lump in my throat.

We returned to the sun porch. Walking out through the front door, I shuffled my feet to warn all the little critters to start packing. It was a relief to breathe in fresh air.

The front yard was shaded with maple and white birch, and scattered throughout were larch trees. Their needles, together with the mulch of fallen leaves from previous years, formed a soft bed. The flat terrain was no comparison for the view from the back door but it was pleasing just the same. It was easy to picture a profusion of flowers blooming around the base of the trees.

"Well, Mr. Howard, you were right. This place is a dump."

"Oh now, I never said such a thing." His blustering reaction to my teasing amused me. "It's a fixer upper. A family could come in here and get quite a bit accomplished in a year or so, if they made an effort."

I counted to ten before I spoke. "So because I'm alone you don't think this is the place for me."

He gave me a suspicious look that became stern as his thick fair brows descended and his eyes disappeared into full cheeks.

We stood facing each other like adversaries about to do battle.

"You don't want this place. There is a house next door that is empty too." He turned, his chin pointing to the dense border. "Someday both these places will be torn down and cabins put up here. Yessir, good spot for cabins."

He gave a jovial nod, turned his back, and headed for the truck. I called after him, my hands fisted at my sides. "Mr. Howard, I've decided to buy this property. The opportunity is too good to pass up. I can restore this house. The maintenance on these two acres is not formidable."

With an abrupt stop, he jerked his body around to face me.

"Even for an old woman living alone." My jaw pulsed with furious resolve. Seeing the flush rise in his already blushing cheeks, I stood erect, determined not to look as scared as I felt. "I'm in good physical shape, Mr. Howard, with energy to spare." I hoped my enthusiasm would convince the both of us.

"Jumpin' Jaysus woman," he stammered. "If you wants it, it's yours." He gesticulated wildly and his accent became even more pronounced. "We'll have to write it up and see about financing since you're a woman on your own and everything. But I don't know why y'ed wants to live out here all alone." He waved his arm, as if dismissing the idea.

Then his bushy brows raised another thought. "This is quite a chunk of money for this property. Does your family know about this? Is there someone you would like to bring out to see the place and maybe give you some advice?"

A grey-blond lock of hair drooped down on his forehead. The genuine look of concern on his full round face deflated my mounting hostility towards him.

This time I was the one to walk away. "The financing, as you call it, will be a certified check. Please find me a local lawyer as I don't have one here. And for the paperwork, make sure the title is clear, and secure a copy of the latest land survey. Someone spent a lot of money here at one time getting the property serviced."

"Yeah, well, it was two brothers, see. That's why these two houses are out here. One feller died and the other one lost his wife then totally lost interest. It was rented out a few times but nobody kept up the rent." The agent was huffing along behind me, trying to keep pace with my long strides. "The family figured it would just get taken over by vagrants if they didn't try to sell it. Actually," he lowered his voice to a confidential tone when he caught up with me, "rumour has it that somebody might be interested in the other place. Somebody from the States."

Raising his voice to a conversational level he continued, "Americans will soon own the lot of us. No doubt it will get torn down and, like I said, a few fancy cabins will go up." He stared out at the dense bank of trees as if imagining the smoke curling out of the chimneys.

Still quite red in the face, he continued in his rapid Newfoundland dialect, even though I was too busy making plans to listen.

Mr. Howard headed to his vehicle, but I walked back to the cliffside, feeling thrilled but nervous at my decision.

When the last lingering doubt vanished, I walked back toward the vehicle taking a deep breath of the moist sea air and pausing to admire the wild landscape. When I climbed into the SUV, the agent gave a slight shake of his head and flicked the truck gear into reverse. He slowly backed out of the driveway and onto the soon-to-be familiar, rutted road.

Certain I would find peace on these two acres, I closed my eyes and surrendered to the moment.

The beginning.

Nancy Kay Clark

"Four Months' Hard Sweeping"—*Neo Opsis Science Fiction Magazine*,
Issue 22, 2012

"The Naming of Things"—*CommuterLit.com*, 2013

Phyllis Humby

"Delusional Date"—*Readings from the Fringe*,
Eden Mills Writers' Festival, 2013

Michael Joll

"In Singapore," "Wilma"—*Perfect Execution and Other Stories*,
Middle Road Publishers, 2017; *CommuterLit.com*, 2013-2014

"With Regret"—*CommuterLit.com*, 2013

Steve Nelson

"Our Plan to Save the World"—*Rathalla Review*, Fall 2015

"Night at the Store"—*Phantasmagoria*, Volume 4, Number 1, 2004

"Maranda on Fire"—*Lunch Ticket*, February 2016

Frank T. Sikora

"Jenny Can't Go Back to Bismarck" and "300 Miles to Leadville"—*The Crooked Edge of Another Day: An Anthology of the Bizarre*, Ascent Aspirations Publishing, 2012

"Hey Miles, What's the Plan?"—*Commuterlit Selections: Fall 2013, A Month of Reading for Your Transit Commute*, 2013

"Bozeman Before the Fire"—*CommuterLit.com*, 2015

Made in the USA
Lexington, KY
05 May 2018